# C.K. STEAD

has published eight novels, two collections of short stories, ten collections of poetry, four of literary criticism, and has edited a number of anthologies. His work is represented in most New Zealand anthologies of poetry and short stories, and he has won a number of awards, including the New Zealand Book Award for fiction, the Jessie Mackay Award for poetry, the New Zealand Book Award for poetry, the Katherine Mansfield short story prize, the Mansfield-Menton Fellowship, and the Arts Council Scholarship in Letters. He was professor of English at Auckland University for twenty years before leaving in 1986 to write full time. In 1984 C.K. Stead was awarded the CBE for services to New Zealand literature; in 1990 he received the Queen's Medal. He is one of only two New Zealand writers to have been elected a Fellow of the Royal Society of Literature.

Stead's novel *Smith's Dream* was made into the movie *Sleeping Dogs* by Roger Donaldson, and he and Donaldson are currently working on a film script of his novel *Villa Vittoria*. His best-known work of literary criticism is *The New Poetic*, which sold over 100,000 copies in Britain and America.

# C.K. STEAD

## The End of the
## CENTURY
## at the End of the
## WORLD

Flamingo
*An Imprint of* HarperCollins*Publishers*

Flamingo
*An imprint of* HarperCollins*Publishers*
First published 1992
This edition published 1999

HarperCollins*Publishers (New Zealand) Limited*
P.O. Box 1, Auckland

ISBN 1 86950 299 X

Printed by Griffin Press, Australia

*To A. S. Byatt in London and*
*P. C. Jersild in Stockholm*

But now there are no more islands to be found
And the eye scans risky horizons of its own
In unsettled weather, and murmurs of the drowned
   Haunt their familiar beaches –
Who navigates us towards what unknown

But not improbable provinces? Who reaches
A future down for us from the high shelf
Of spiritual daring? Not those speeches
   Pinning on the past like a decoration
For merit that congratulates itself.

O not the self-important celebration
Or most painstaking history, can release
The current of a discoverer's elation
   And silence the voices saying,
"Here is the world's end where wonders cease."

ALLEN CURNOW

# ONE

# 1990 – At the Bay

Aprils bring birthdays, and memories of birthdays – "his and hers" (his and mine). They bring Dan Cooper back into my life, just briefly, touch-and-go, if not as a name on a card, then as a voice on the phone; never, or never until now, as a visitor. But I will come to that.

My name is Laura Vine Barber, 26 Rangiview Crescent, Eastern Bays, Auckland.

I run that through my mind in the way my children do when they go on to add "New Zealand, the World, the Universe, Space".

What else? Married to lawyer Roger Marley Barber, three children (Angela, Ben, Jacob). Housewife, and in the past eighteen months, postgraduate student enrolled to do research on "Auckland's North Shore before the Harbour Bridge, and its Role in the Creation of a Distinct New Zealand Literature". Supervisor, Steve Casey (Professor).

I didn't, and don't, like the thesis jargon. How does a place have "a role in the creation" of something? What is "a distinct New Zealand Literature"?

"Never mind," Steve Casey says, smiling his tranquillizing smile. "That's just the bullshit part. Let's get it past the Academic Committee and then we can begin to make something of it."

I don't mind that he says "we". I'm glad of it. I need encouragement. Steve and I were students together. He was always brilliant, radical, sexy, and heading somewhere, like a fast train through a beautiful landscape . . .

But wait. That sly image of the train, which came in the instant of my thinking about him, tells as much about me as about Steve. There's an invitation in it to see him as *too* fast, getting to the end of the line too soon, seeing nothing but the track, while I make my way appreciatively through that beautiful landscape, by car, or bicycle, or on foot.

The truth is that twenty years ago Steve made me feel subordinate. He got A grades, he made notable speeches in the student forum, he appeared not to hear anything I said that was in the least serious and then would prove a week later, by referring to it (and probably dismissing it) that he'd heard and thought about it. He went away on a scholarship, wrote a thesis with the title "Ambiguous Signs: the Sexuality of Marxism in British Poetry of the 1930s and '40s", came back a lecturer, and rose quickly to his present eminence.

The problem has been mine, not his. I was uncertain – still am. Without him I would never have begun to climb this ladder, which I see as quite different from his. His was stainless steel; mine's rope – a ladder up out of the pit.

Why these images (trains, ladders)? And how unfair to my married life as it has been to describe it as a pit. But isn't there something pit-like about even the best of domestic lives? Can't that be said without maligning one's family, or doing less than justice to one's circumstances?

This morning I dropped Angela and Ben at school and took Jacob on down to the crèche. He seems to like it. As I carry him up the wooden ramp his legs start going, and when I put him down he heads for the sand like a little robot. I never handed Angie or Ben over to others' care at such an early age. I can't see – not rationally – any reason for guilt or anxiety. But when I give the women his red and white striped bag with JACOB in big blue letters I feel a wrench, as if I'm abandoning him.

It's late summer/early autumn – the sky clear, the sea

windless. The dark rough texture of Rangitoto, alight in shades of dark green and black, makes seeing seem like touching. On the headland toi-toi puts its white feather dusters up against the blue. I watch Jacob making a road in the sand with his tractor. I turn on the ramp to look up at the suburb, its houses angled this way and that to get a view of the bay. I can pick out our house, and above it and away to the left, the cottage where Dan Cooper's aunt Amelia – the writer Hilda Tapler as she called herself – lived and wrote her novel *Nor Question Much*. As I've worked on my thesis subject, and found her papers deposited in the university library, my sights have narrowed on her. So my topic has been expanded: "With Special Attention to the Life and Work of Hilda Tapler".

"Bye, Jacob." I feel honour-bound not to sneak off. If his face were to crumple into tears, I feel I should see it. I hope for a smile. He frowns, and goes back to pushing his tractor along the sandpit road, puckering his lips and blowing to make engine noises.

The gate shuts behind me with a well-oiled double-click. I feel it physically. I'm sure if I should hear it at some time in the future I will get a faint but deep-seated sense of wrongdoing.

Back at the house there are temptations. To sit on the verandah and do nothing. Or housekeeping – bedrooms, kitchen, the ironing. Then there's something that doesn't tempt – just happens. You drift in the unfamiliar silence, doing many things (picking objects up in one place, putting them down in another) but nothing purposeful, while thoughts come and go like clouds across the isthmus. Time passes and leaves no memory.

So I unpack my thesis notes and spread them out on the big table that looks towards the sea. I feel relaxed, but with a faint tinge of anxiety. It's a mood in which, years ago, I would have begun to write – fictions that were diaries, diaries that were fiction. But I grew out of writing as therapy without ever growing into it as anything else. That's why the chance to study the work and private papers of Hilda Tapler has been so exciting. And it has given my own suburb an atmosphere, an interest, a history, which it lacked before. I can look up from the photocopy of a manuscript knowing that in front of me is the same scene the writer looked out on when she lifted her eyes from the same piece of writing.

Recently I had a dream unlike any I've ever had, because I was nowhere in it, not even a passive observer. It was a story, partly watched, as in a movie theatre, partly understood, almost like an abstract idea. A young woman had fallen in love with an older woman. There was no suggestion of sex. It was just love. Told of this, the older woman thought about it and then suggested the younger one should give her ten thousand dollars. The young woman worked for many years (how did years pass in a dream? I don't know, but they did) saving most of what she earned. At last she had the money and took it, in banknotes in a suitcase, to the older woman, who accepted it. That was all. Nothing was offered in return.

The end came as such a surprise it made me laugh. Laughing woke me, and I lay there wondering where in my mind was the hidden part that could tell a story that would give me such a surprise.

A night or two later it returned, but changed. The older woman accepted the suitcase and shut the door. The young woman went away bitter and angry – but after a time she smiled. The story, which had turned momentarily cold, became warm again. Half awake now, I put my own interpretation on that smile. It was because really each woman had made the other a gift. The young woman had given the money. The older had made it possible for the younger to give something to the only person she really loved.

But there wasn't the same satisfaction there had been with

the first version – the one I think of as pure dream. Intellect had got into it – and explanation.

Last week, having coffee with Steve Casey, I told him about it. We were sitting in the sun outside the Student Union. He leaned back in his chair and smiled. "You know what it means, of course."

Of course? Of course I didn't. Did he?

Steve told me I was the younger woman. The older one was Hilda Tapler. My thesis was the ten thousand dollars.

So there it was again – the fast train already fuming in the station (I thought of it as Paris Nord, never having set foot in France) while I was still cycling through the wheat fields and along the leafy lanes. Yes, dammit (and "of course") I found his interpretation convincing. I was glad of it, couldn't reject it, wouldn't want not to have heard it. But I liked, and still do, the poor child of my own brain better than the wonder-child of his. To be more exact, I hold to that moment of surprise when I woke laughing and understood nothing.

Sometimes I wonder whether instead of taking up research I ought to have gone back to writing things of my own. I feel such affinity with the notes Hilda Tapler made planning and working on her fiction. But a return to university is something everyone understands. To have said, "I'm going to *write*," would have sounded pretentious, even to myself.

Tomorrow is my birthday. As I look down the street, expecting to see the postman, some lines from a poem by G. M. Hopkins come into my head:

why must
Disappointment all I endeavour end?
Wert thou my enemy, O thou my friend,
How wouldst thou worse, I wonder, than thou dost
Defeat, thwart me?

13

I remember quoting them at Dan Cooper when we quarrelled. Or did he quote them at me? We all remake our memories, rewrite history to suit ourselves – so let's say Dan and I took turns to quote them at one another . . .

I take my mind away from that and go back to reading the draft of an unfinished story among Hilda Tapler's papers. It's about a sexual encounter; and although the details are not as physical as they might be in a story written in 1990, they're more graphic than a similar scene in her novel, *Nor Question Much*, which at the time of publication seemed shocking enough. In the story the man is forcing himself on the narrator, who seems indistinguishable from Hilda. She seems to want this attack as confirmation of something, even at the same time she tries to repel it; and it arouses an excitement that's unmistakable in the writing.

I would like to make something of this scene in my thesis, discover how it relates to events in the author's life; but when I mentioned it to Steve last week he looked doubtful and said, "Dangerous ground". I suppose my disappointment showed, because he added, "It's up to you, of course."

Of course.

I see the postie coming up the hill. By the time she reaches the gate I'm already there, waiting. It takes only a moment, walking back up the path, to check that among the letters there's nothing with that green "House of Representatives" stamp that means it comes from Dan Cooper. I feel an old irritation – with myself, but also with Dan. He's the one who has created this annual crisis by always sending something on, or just before, my birthday – card, telegram, book, small memento or postcard from a foreign place. Always discreet, in good taste, and with a message that's subtle, ambiguous, teasing, affectionate, reminding. I've reacted differently from year to year – sometimes amused, sometimes indifferent, just occasionally regretful.

Is it ever possible to break right away from the first person you really fall in love with? That's a question Hilda Tapler's

14

fiction asks – one of her themes – and another reason for my interest. So many years after Dan and I went our separate ways, why is there still this unwelcome anticipation that threatens to spoil my birthday? I have to conceal it from Roger – but it hasn't been possible to conceal it altogether. Roger is confident, dependable, but he's not unshakeable.

And then there's an argument I have with myself about Dan's motive. Does he know what he's doing? Has he always known? It seems innocent enough, even proper, not to cut yourself off from someone you once loved. But there's something insinuating about the way the greetings come, and the precision with which they land right on, or just before, the day. They lay claim to me. They're an intrusion.

Wert thou my enemy, O thou my friend
How would thou worse, I wonder, than thou dost?

Often the messages involve numbers. Dan's birthday and mine are in April – mine on the 8th, his on the 17th. He used to point out that in the April when I turned eight on the eighth, he turned 17 on the seventeenth; and that our ages in years, added until they produced a single digit, have been the same since I had my first birthday and he had his tenth, and would continue to be until the end of time. Because of this, he said, I would always be able to work out his age, and he mine. So this month, for example, I will be 38 (3 + 8 = 11; 1 + 1 = 2) and he 47 (4 + 7 = 11; 1 + 1 = 2). This primitive numerology, which he invokes sometimes by patterns on an otherwise letterless birthday card, has the power to make me at least irritable, sometimes downright angry. It strikes me as pointless, meaningless, silly. But it's also inescapable, remorseless, and – "numinous" is the word that comes to mind. Every year it lays a ghostly hand on me.

I go back indoors and return to Hilda Tapler. Dan has

been absent from my life a very long time, and he's certainly not wanted back; but even in his absence, he's dependable. If there's nothing from him today, that means it will arrive tomorrow, bang on my birthday.

★    ★    ★

I have a strong impulse (one I may yet give in to) to tell it like a story – beginning, let's say, "On the night of . . ."

For example:

On the night of Laura Barber's 38th birthday her husband Roger took her out for dinner at the restaurant upstairs in the old Ferry Building. It was a mild night and they were able to sit out of doors on the terrace and watch boats coming and going on the harbour. It had been such an awful day she didn't want to talk about it. She talked instead about her research. Yesterday she'd discovered a diary entry in which Hilda Tapler had described giving lunch to Frank Sargeson and Robin Hyde. The three writers had laughed about the fact that they all used *noms de plume* – Frank Sargeson born Norris Davy, Robin Hyde born Iris Wilkinson, and Hilda Tapler born Amelia Henryson. Like Katherine Mansfield, Sargeson had taken his mother's name – but not, he insisted, out of piety or respect. "When she dies," he'd said, "I'm going to dance on her grave."

Roger frowned, and shook his head. "Writers!"

The wine was open, their soup plates removed, and they were waiting for their main courses. Roger's forearm rested on the table and his fingers lay lightly on Laura's hand. She thought how handsome he looked – his pale, springy hair brushed down not altogether successfully, its health and vigour only temporarily constrained – and she surprised herself, not for the first time, with the thought that he should have married someone more suitable.

She wanted to ask what he meant by that exclamation, "Writers!", but checked herself. So many things these days

16

were irritations, pin-pricks – and of course she knew what he meant. To want to dance on your mother's grave – it was a failure of piety to think it, and of propriety to say it. Not that Roger would have expressed himself so loftily. He would have said, probably, with the dismissive shrug of a man who lived and worked in a world of law and commerce, that writers were a flaky lot.

To which she might have replied that of course it was deplorable, but it had made her laugh out loud.

It occurred to her that a lot of her conversation with Roger went on in her head, and got no further. It's called marriage, she thought, and smiled – a smile he responded to with an expression which seemed to ask what she was finding amusing at the same time that it revealed his expectation that he wouldn't be told.

So there was a silence, and they looked away from one another, out to the harbour. That was the great advantage of open-air eating. You were not forced upon one another quite so relentlessly.

"Well," he said at last, in a tone so casual it seemed anything but. "Did he send you something?"

"Dan?" She thought she fielded it rather well. But then, maybe he thought he'd sounded casual. She shook her head. "Nothing."

"Not even . . ."

Not even what? What third alternative was there between "something" and "nothing"? "Nothing," she repeated. And she added, because she felt her irritation had shown itself: "Here's to a Dan-less birthday."

He said he would drink to that, and they clinked their glasses. But he couldn't let it rest there. "It's odd, isn't it? He's always been so . . ."

She supposed it was her frown checked him. "Dependable, you mean?"

He stared at his glass. "Yes," he said. "Something like that."

17

Dan's refusal ever to quite go away had been a nuisance. It had never occurred to Laura until today that his annual demonstration that there was someone "out there" who valued her had given her a kind of strength. Had Roger's shadowy competitor at last given up the fight?

She thought of saying that Dan had bigger fish to fry now, other irons in the fire. She had in mind his new role as Cabinet Minister; but the fish and the irons got cancelled before they were uttered. "I imagine he's busy," she said, and thought how lame that sounded.

But it was a useful trigger. Roger was away now, talking about the Government's problems. The split between Labour's right and left wings was widening. There was a rumour that the Prime Minister might be challenged in Caucus. And there was the Maori problem. Maori claims for land, fishing rights, mining rights, even for a share in the air waves – they were stacking up before the Waitangi Tribunal, making Labour unpopular. "Labour bought this lot," Roger said. "They gave the Tribunal too much clout."

She sipped her wine, letting it lie on her tongue inside closed lips, and watched a ferry angling into the wharf, the gang-plank going down, the few passengers straggling ashore.

Roger was reminiscing now about some Maori land near his uncle's house, just out of Tauranga. "Those people could have had a dairy farm, orchards, kiwi fruit, but they did nothing – just lived there in shacks, grew a few kumaras, picked puha, went fishing, and went into town for work when it suited them, or to collect a pension. Finally they sold to a developer. Now it's a suburb – all good housing, all with harbour views. Their kids or their grandchildren will say they were robbed and want it back. But the truth is, they sold up and went."

Laura nodded. She didn't want to have that old argument

again. Roger was a lawyer and thought there must always be a verdict – guilty, or not guilty. To her it just seemed there was a history, much of it sad.

"I haven't told you," she said. "I've discovered something new about Hilda Tapler."

His frown faded. He was glad of a way out of that subject which seemed these days both to bore and to obsess him.

"She was fascinated by Katherine Mansfield. That's not surprising. A lot of people have been – especially writers. But in the 1950s Hilda wrote an account of meeting her, interviewing her – here in New Zealand. It's fiction. Well – she doesn't say so, but it has to be. Otherwise you have to believe that Katherine faked her own death at Fontainebleau in 1923 and then took a new name, Katya Lawrence, and returned to live in New Zealand. And that she never revealed the truth to anyone until she met Hilda."

"Is that possible?"

"No. Well, possible – yes. Hilda's account of their meeting's very convincing. It's full of detail. But that just means it's good fiction."

"Or the truth?"

"I wish it was. What a find that would be!"

Good food, good wine, the view of the harbour, had their combined effect. Laura relaxed. So did Roger. They talked like old friends. His hair sprang free of its gel and caught the light behind his head. She thought again how handsome he looked.

Idly she wondered whether studying a group of writers had the effect of making you think as they did. Frank Sargeson, she'd discovered, had liked to label things he disapproved of "bourgeois", which according to Hilda's journal he pronounced "boogeois". Sargeson, Laura thought, would have dismissed her and Roger, their comfortable house, their two cars and three children, as

19

"boogeois". Still, she would have liked to have met the man who would say aloud that when his mother died he was going to dance on her grave.

*     *     *

Why had it been, at least until our dinner on that terrace, "an awful day"? Briefly, it had gone as follows:

> My birthday began with the water-
> Birds and the birds of the winged trees flying my name
> Above the farms and the white horses . . .

No, that was Dylan Thomas, and another echo coming into my waking head from long ago. My birthday began with the alarm clock, and the children, marshalled and coached by Roger, bringing presents and singing "Happy Birthday" almost in tune. I hugged them one by one and all together, and unwrapped what they'd brought while they stood over me, enjoying my displays of enthusiasm and astonishment.

After that it was the usual morning, the usual scrimmage – getting Roger away, Angie and Ben to school, Jacob to the crèche (a smile this time from the sandpit roadworks), and finally my car to the workshop for repairs.

Do I need to give you (you? myself? who is out there anyway?) the details of my day? The point is that as the time for the post approached, I found myself tense and distracted – and then disconcerted that I should be.

I made my way through some pages of the difficult writing in which Hilda Tapler had recorded her "interview" with Katherine Mansfield, but I took in only a little. My eyes strayed to my watch, and down the street. The postie was late. Or had she gone by unnoticed? I went down to the gate and waited. She came into view – yes, there she was – and went by without stopping. I was so surprised, so disbelieving, I called after her, in a voice that didn't sound like my own, "Nothing for 26?"

She checked the bunch of letters in her hand, flipped the lid of her bag and looked inside. "Nothing," she said.

Going back up the path, I argued with myself. It wasn't just that there was nothing from Dan. Surely there was always something in the mail. I couldn't remember a day when nothing came. If there had been just one item – a bill, a brochure, anything at all – I'm sure I would have been less troubled. It was as if the sun hadn't come up.

I made coffee, tried to be brisk, and found myself wiping the stove-top, the bench, the kitchen table. I stacked dishes in the machine, put bread in the bin and milk in the refrigerator. In the living room I tidied magazines and newspapers, picked up toys, occupied myself.

I must have got myself back to my work table, and later stopped for lunch, which I ate listening to a Brahms symphony. After that there was time for more work but I went into the bedroom and lay down. The shafts of April sunlight came in on an angle. Motes drifted in them. There was a faint sheen of dust on the mirror and through it I could see, reflected, long heavy boughs of the pohutukawa outside the window . . .

I was woken by the phone ringing. As I went to it I looked at the time. It was already past the hour when I was to pick Jacob up from the crèche. An unfamiliar voice was asking something. It wasn't the crèche and I hung up.

So you have to see me hot and rumpled, rushing to put myself together and get where I was supposed to be – a mess, or feeling one, though of course in reality hair was brushed, makeup applied, clothes straightened. This was no madwoman rushing out into the street "with my hair down, so"; only an average harassed housewife, averagely late to collect her child, but one whose day had left her badly flustered.

There wasn't time to get my car from the workshop. I

took the pushchair and hurried, breaking into an idiot half-run, down towards the bay.

As the crèche gate closed behind me with its accusatory double-click, one of the minders appeared on the ramp. She was carrying Jacob. He was smiling, and looked so lovely . . . Does it need saying? There was chocolate around his mouth and down the front of his shirt. As I took him, acknowledging lateness, apologizing, he put a small, welcome chocolate hand into my hair.

The young woman was very nice, very kind. Jacob had been a happy boy, she told me. He'd slept an hour after lunch. I told her I had slept too; and then, feeling that this needed explanation, "It's my birthday."

I dumped him into his pushchair without doing up the harness, and manoeuvred through the gate she was holding open for me.

We were heading downhill to the workshop when a jogger came towards us wearing bright orange running gear, the wires of a walkman going in under his headband. As he panted by, Jacob stood up and twisted round in his chair to watch. I stopped, reaching forward to grab him – but too suddenly. He pitched forward on to the gravel pavement. There was a sickening moment in which he seemed to free fall, and then the thump of his forehead striking the ground, his head twisting sideways as he rolled.

Why should I say at once whether serious damage was done? The gap between seeing him fall and knowing he wasn't dead, or likely to be, seemed so much longer than any paragraph could occupy, how can three sentences do it justice? I was to blame, and for my carelessness had to endure that eternity of a split second in which consequences were uncertain.

I dived to pick him up and the pushchair rolled away on an angle and came to a stop in a hedge. He was yelling now. There are occasions when a yell is welcome, and this was one. There was a graze on his forehead, a small cut on his nose, a trickle of blood-and-chocolate down one cheek.

I hugged him, holding him tight. I cared about nothing else – what came or didn't come in the mail, who loved or had loved whom and why they had parted. Jacob was for this instant (I'm sorry to be lyrical/hysterical) my only and proper concern, my little planet – hurt, howling, indignant, alive. Now perhaps, after all, the birds of the winged trees were flying my name above the farms and the white horses . . .

After a few long minutes he was quiet, taking deep sobbing breaths that made his whole body shudder. His eyes were alert – I could see no sign of concussion.

Still he clung to me, didn't want to go back into his pushchair. Somehow I wheeled it with one hand, holding him on my hip with the other. My arm ached. My heart pounded.

*    *    *

We had parked at Devonport and come over to the restaurant by ferry, just for the ride. Returning, I told Roger how romantic the North Shore had seemed before the building of the Harbour Bridge – that's to say, the North Shore as I found it in my writers. Roger (is it a little retrospective stab of malice that I record it?) talked about property values, and what the Bridge had done for them.

When we got into his car it didn't start first time, and I knew he was pleased. It gave him a chance to say again how much he would like to buy a BMW. I didn't respond, which was a response in itself. This was a continuing battle, one I knew I was going to lose.

I told him I was worried about Jacob. His bruises might have disturbed his sleep; the memory of his fall might have given him nightmares. It was true; it was also a way out of the BMW argument, and nothing more was said.

And when we got home everything was quiet. Jacob had let out a few yelps, Ginny Scobie reported; but only in his sleep. Angie and Ben had given her no trouble. All was well.

I made tea and brought it in. Roger was sitting beside Ginny on the couch. She was telling him about a programme she'd watched on the subject of what she called "race rels". He was smiling, watching her talk as much as listening to what she said.

He likes her, I thought.

And she liked him. It was as if I was seeing a more open, less anxious man, one who with me had become cautious, nervous of making a wrong move. Yes, I felt guilty – but that wasn't new.

When he got up to drive her home I was suddenly convinced they were having an affair. Through the door I could just see him helping her into the jacket she'd left in the hallway. What came into my mind was the ending of a story by Katherine Mansfield, in which a woman, watching through an open door, sees her husband saying goodbye to their guest and recognizes that he is telling her he loves her. But Roger's lips didn't move until he called back over his shoulder, "Back soon, darling."

While he was gone I walked up and down feeling surges of anger and then of self-reproach. I had never loved him enough, or as he deserved to be loved. But then I thought, even if I'd failed in some ways, so had he. How could he be so irresponsible when we had three small children? What would happen to me? How could I cope?

I imagined him kissing Ginny, winding his finger into her hair . . . My mind shuddered away from it.

When I heard his car in the drive only a quarter of an hour had passed. He came in, staring down at his key-ring, and then looked up and saw me standing in the middle of the sitting room. His faint smile faded.

"Hullo," he said. "Why are you standing there?"

There was still something of that relaxed innocence I'd seen when he was talking to Ginny.

24

"What's going on, Roger?" I heard the peculiar harshness of my own voice. He blinked and said nothing.

"Between you and Ginny."

"I drove her home. What do you mean?"

"You're having an affair." Even as I said it, I knew it wasn't true.

"With Ginny? Jesus, Laura . . ."

"I'm sorry. I . . ."

"Ginny's a baby. And I don't . . ."

My eyes filled with tears. Relief? Yes. Shame? Certainly. But there was also something strange and disconcerting, something like regret, as if there was a craving in me for pain.

I said I was sorry. He put his arms around me. "We'd better find another baby-sitter. A male . . ."

"Not a male. But a big ugly one would be nice. Ginny's too pretty – and too clever."

"She's clever – that's true."

"And she likes you too much."

He looked interested, as if that was something that hadn't crossed his mind.

\*     \*     \*

I was sitting in the sun in the quadrangle with Steve Casey. He stretched his arms above his head and yawned up at the sky. He was tired. Overworked. Too many committees. Too many essays to mark.

But he'd found time to read my summary of the work I'd done. He said it was good, it was interesting, it was useful. "I knew once you got into it you'd find something."

I noticed he said "you" now, not "we", and I was glad of that.

It was a long time since we'd been students together, and we hadn't met often in the intervening years, but now we seemed to be falling back into the old easy-going way with one another. And if I still felt subordinate, that wasn't inappropriate. He was a professor, and my supervisor.

I think I admired his mind quite as much as I ever had, but now I felt a certain detachment, a sort of female-to-male indulgence towards what I thought of as his intellectual fads.

He was making no attempt to force me into his own Post-Structuralist modes of thought. That too was good, even if it was because he thought me incapable of mastering them. If that was indeed the reason (of course he never said so) he was right; but I wasn't sure whether it was because of an intellectual disability or simply the quickness of my mind to reject what it had no appetite or use for.

I was explaining to him in more detail Hilda Tapler's account of her meetings with the woman who went by the name of Katya Lawrence and who claimed to be Katherine Mansfield – telling him how convincing it seemed, and how detailed it was in its names and dates and places. What I couldn't decide was whether Hilda had meant to pass it off as true, or whether she thought everyone would understand it was fiction. And then sometimes it crossed my mind to wonder whether it really was true – that Katherine Mansfield had not died in 1923 but had lived to a ripe old age at home in New Zealand.

According to Hilda's account of what she'd been told, Gurdjieff, Katherine's famous guru, had insisted that she "must die in order to live". If she was to shake off the tuberculosis that was killing her she must rid herself of the name, the personality, the identity – which meant also the written work – to which the disease had attached itself. Leaving that self behind, she would leave her disease behind as well. She'd done this first at Gurdjieff's Institute for the Harmonious Development of Man at Fontainebleau. Once that first stage was complete, Katherine was so impressed by the miracle of renewed health that she was ready for anything. So now her "death" had to be arranged. It

26

involved the complicity of a very few people at the Institute, of her friend Ida Baker, and of her estranged husband, John Middleton Murry. Ida Baker was (as Katherine had sometimes said) her "slave". She could be relied upon for anything. Murry had complied because he knew the marriage was over. He had nothing to lose, and something to gain. Alive, Katherine had eluded him. In death he could claim her as his own for ever, and did, first by ordering a headstone to be inscribed, "Katherine Mansfield, wife to John Middleton Murry", followed by lines from Shakespeare about plucking the flower Safety from the nettle Danger – which in the light of Hilda Tapler's story took on a secret significance.

"After all," I said to Steve, "you don't really pluck safety from danger by dying, do you?"

He laughed. "On the whole not, I'd say."

Steve had a lecture coming up on the hour. There wasn't time to give him more detail. But I assured him it all fitted together. If Hilda had made it up it was a marvellous play on real life – like a huge pun.

"Work on it as fiction," was Steve's advice. "It has to be a fiction."

I thought so too, but I felt a need to prove it. Steve saw everything as theory. He liked the idea of it, and didn't care about the facts, whereas for me it was entirely a question of fact. Either Katherine Mansfield had died in 1923, or she had pretended to die, and it was important to know which.

★   ★   ★

My name was Laura Vine Jackson, daughter of Vincent E. and Camilla Jackson, and now popularly or suburbanly known as Mrs Roger Barber, 26 Rangiview Crescent, Auckland/Tamaki Makau-Rau, North Island/Te Ika a Maui, New Zealand/Aotearoa, the World/Te Ao Marama. Why are our names so precious and so insecure, so serious and so funny? Is it an aspect of time and place, or of all times and all places? In these winds, surrounded by these waters, do we hang on more desperately and less successfully? Is this my problem, or a national malaise? Today, alas (according to the *Herald*) died Smiley Tania Mefanwy Urban, aged two. I know nothing more than her name, but it takes hold. I say it over and over, like a poem, as I used to say in the third-form, not thinking about or caring what it might mean, "The protozoan amoeba respires by simple diffusion through the cell walls." What is wrong with the head-workings of Laura Vienna Jolly Rogerson, who once tried to write a novel (yes, we will come to it) in which she called herself "Larissa", and Dan "Dave", and Roger "Larry", and Maurice Scobie "Manning Strettor", but who stuck on her stubborn flatmate Caroline, baulked of invention, and could call her nothing but "Caroline"? Is writing ("serious" writing, you understand, Oh God!) only the equivalent of putting stones around the edges of the tent as a storm comes up? "Don't be mistaken, Lord. Don't let your weak old eyes deceive you. This is not a tent. This is rock, steel, adamant . . ." *WHACK*! Am I sane, down here in the pit, putting a hand and a foot on the rope ladder, staring up at the stars? Amelia Henryson becomes Hilda Tapler. Norris Davy (and who can blame him? – it was, as he said, "a shit of a name") becomes Frank Sargeson. Iris Wilkinson becomes Robin Hyde. Is this "the North Shore's role in the Creation of a Distinct New Zealand Literature"? This shifting of names? This moving of the ground under our feet? And elsewhere, earlier, Kathleen Beauchamp becomes Katherine Mansfield becomes (does she? does she?) Katya Lawrence. Where is the begetting in all this, as in the Biblical "Maurice Scobie begat Terry Scobie who begat Ginny Scobie . . ." Beautiful, dangerous Ginny, who will beget whom? and with whom? Or is it only fathers beget? – in which case we must rephrase it: Beautiful, dangerous Ginny, with whom who will beget whom? There is a destiny which shapes our grammar as it shapes our naming. Help me, Oh spirit of Steve Casey, great white theorist of the white lie of language, Why am I here (Waiamaihea?), with my three little ones, on a volcanic isthmus only a tick of the geological clock from the next eruption? Rangitoto ("bloody sky" – so someone was around to see it and to name it) was the last: it sits there in my window, silent, dark reminder, Madame Defarge of the Hauraki Gulf, making such a discreet and threatening spectacle of itself.

> Not mine own fears, nor the prophetic soul
> Of the wide world dreaming on things to come,
> Can yet the lease of my true love control . . .

Turn off your mind machine, Laura. Get on with your word-work.

*       *       *

17 April, 1990, nine days after her birthday: Laurapunzel Barber is working at the big table. There are Mansfield books piled up and spread around her – biographies, memoirs, selections of letters and journals. She is trying to decide whether Hilda Tapler, when she put aside the preoccupations that came to a head in her novel, *Nor Question Much*, and turned to the subject of Katherine Mansfield, was writing fact, or using facts to create a new fiction.

The Indian summer is persisting. The air is still, the sky blue, and white clouds hang about in it like suburban washing. A big beige-coloured car comes into view, moving slowly. It has a small metal flag-post over the front fender, but no flag. As it gets closer Laura can see the driver, wearing a uniform cap, looking out at street numbers. He turns and says something to his passenger. The car turns right, speeding up a little, and runs down towards the bay.

Laura watches it go. For a long time she stares down the hill where it vanished. At last a figure appears, a man in a dark suit, walking up the hill. He wears tinted glasses, which combine with his formal suit and tie to make him faintly sinister, and therefore conspicuous when perhaps he means not to be.

When he reaches her house he checks the number on the gate, looks up at the windows seeing nothing, she supposes, but the reflection of sky and cloud, and walks up the path. There is a brief pause before the door bell rings. Laura sits quite still. She is not making any sort of calculation, not even thinking, simply waiting to see what she will do. After a decent pause the bell rings again. She remains seated. Seconds pass. She thinks how quiet everything is, and then recognizes that what she thought of as silence allows her, if she concentrates, to distinguish the kzaaa kzaaa of cicadas, a baby crying in a nearby house, starlings scrambling on the iron roof, a car climbing the hill, distant hammering. The air is so still it seems for a moment that these – especially the cicada sounds – hurt her ears.

Her visitor presses the bell-push a third time, a perhaps disappointed or irritable stab at it, and at once turns away. She hears his footsteps. He comes into sight, walking back down the path. It's only as he reaches the gate and pulls it open that she finds herself standing, leaning across the table to push open the window.

"Dan!"

He turns and smiles, pulling off his shades. "Oh, so you're there. Can I come up?"

Up? Should she let down her hair?

*     *     *

I think I could reconstruct most of what Dan and I said to one another that day – not surprising, because although his

30

visit was brief and I suppose unremarkable, it was the longest time we'd spent alone together in seventeen years. It was strange to be looking into that doubly familiar face – familiar privately as Dan, publicly as a member of the Government.

I'm sure I greeted him awkwardly. It was hard to know what note to strike. I was pleased to see him, but I think – at first, anyway – I concealed it. And he, too, seemed shy. So at the door we stepped around one another – there was no hug, not even a shaking of hands, which I suppose might have seemed too formal and therefore worse than nothing. And while this strange *pas de deux* went on, two mature adults displaying less than mastery of the moment, I was nevertheless registering something familiar, likeable, and half-forgotten about Dan – that at close quarters I could read him, and see him reading me, without mistakes, or anyway with confidence. Which perhaps explains why I didn't feel much troubled by our awkwardness. It was a sign of something better than indifference.

Shown into the sitting room, he walked around looking at the pictures, at the view from the front windows, at the books spread out on my table. Though we had run into one another from time to time at parties and in public places over the years, he had only once before been to the house – and I thought it certain he remembered that long-ago occasion as clearly as I did. He'd either been a little less than sober, or else gripped by a mood of extravagant nostalgia and regret, and had hardly got into the room before he was trying to kiss me. I had backed away and knocked a pottery vase from the coffee table. This had had the effect of concentrating his mind. He'd focused his attention on picking up every last shard, and rushed away saying it would be replaced. Of course it never was, and that visit had neither been repeated nor mentioned in our subsequent conversations.

But I suppose it explained why he should be giving me

a wide berth, as if to say, Please don't be apprehensive. I'm not going to assault you.

And as I took all this in I was feeling the stirrings of an old affection, and wanting to say, as I might have said long ago, Dan, stop *prowling*, for God's sake. Come here and kiss me.

But it was important that there shouldn't be another embarrassment. I suggested coffee. In fact I said "Coffee, then?" to which he responded "Coffee *now*!"; and the question and answer echoed something out of our past, so that we both smiled at the recognition without, I think, either of us being sure what it was.

He followed me into the kitchen while I made it. Mostly I had my back to him; and then, without thinking (was it quite without thinking?) I asked him to pass me something down from a high shelf, and as he did, there was again such an amused smile passed between us – another moment of familiarity taking us by surprise.

As he handed me whatever it was, he asked, "Am I welcome?"

I said I thought I was pleased to see him. "So far," I added. And then, because even as a joke that seemed gratuitous: "It's your birthday."

I'm sure he was pleased I remembered; but he hastened to assure me that it wasn't why he was visiting. This sounded for a moment so properly ministerial I did, after all, going past him on my way back into the sitting room, and protected by the tray I was holding, plant a brief kiss on his cheek. "Happy Birthday, Dan," I said.

He told me then that he'd got his secretary to phone me on mine, but that I'd hung up before she could put him on the line.

It must have been the call and the strange voice that had woken me from my unscheduled sleep. I said, "I'd told *my* secretary that I wouldn't be taking calls."

He sat in a deep chair and wrapped his arms around his

torso, smiling up at me. "I'm not wearing a flak jacket," he said.

I ignored that, though I registered it as a mild rebuke.

"So if it's not a birthday visit," I said (I was pouring the coffee now), "what brings you?"

At first he was vague, as if he didn't know, or didn't know how best to answer. He was "in the area". He always thought of me in April – "the cruellest month . . . That sort of thing." And then, self-mocking: "No good reason. A lingering passion. Nostalgia."

I said it sounded like opening the bottom drawer.

He acknowledged that. "Down among the moth-balls." But the amused tone vanished and I knew – felt it instantly – that he was on the brink of saying something I would rather not hear. I tried somehow to busy myself with my cup, to deflect it, but it came out just the same. "It's a compulsion," he said. "I just . . . I can't *not* – you know?"

I wondered what he was talking about. It wasn't as if he'd made a habit of it. Was he confusing me with someone else? Or making a general statement about the visits he paid to former lovers? It was in my mind to tell him I hoped he hadn't turned up at my door because his private life had taken a turn for the worse. But that would have been too rough, too personal, undeserved.

"You don't know this," he went on, "but when you and Roger were first married I used to . . . No, let me phrase that more accurately. There were one or two occasions when I came here at night . . ."

"At night? You mean . . ."

"I stood out there in the garden and watched you two through the windows."

I was shocked, of course, and must have shown it, because he rushed to assure me that it was at times when we were eating meals, doing the dishes, watching television – ordinary things.

33

He stared into his coffee. "What's that sound like to you, Laura? I've never been sure you understood how I . . ."

I took the shortest cut I could to deal with it and said it sounded like living dangerously.

He got up and looked again at the view – or was it just for a way of escape? We were both disconcerted by this momentary opening of a door that ought to have remained shut.

When he seemed to have recovered his composure I changed the subject, asked him about the corridors of power, said I hadn't had a chance to congratulate him on becoming a Cabinet Minister.

And so for a time we talked about his life in politics. He told me the excitement of being a Minister was wearing off, replaced by a grinding sense of hard work and imminent defeat. He would have liked to have been in Cabinet during Labour's first term. Now he was in, but the opinion polls were bad. "We're on our way to the meat works. As soon as Lange and Douglas split, everything split – Cabinet, Caucus, the party, the country. It was a disaster. The stock-market crash did it – and then I think Lange lost his nerve."

I asked did he feel like giving up, and he said no, but it got harder.

"With age," I said, and then apologized. "That's an unkind thing to say on your birthday."

"Especially this one – my forty-seventh. The sevens are hardest to take – don't you find? It's because they're so close to the round number – it feels worse than when you get there. Forty-seven feels like fifty – but too soon. Old before my time."

But now he noticed my blank expression, and he laughed. "I'm sorry, Laura. It's what you used to call my numbers-speak."

"Did I? Well, anyway, Dan, however you feel, you don't look it."

"My age? My critics tell me I should *act* it."

34

"You can ignore them, can't you?"

"Yes and no. I've thought lately if I'm going to stay in politics I need to get back to first base."

I wondered what that might be. The Anarchist coffee bar which he'd run when we first met? But he said no to that. "And not Marx – not in 1990. I was thinking of those old lefties like Maurice Scobie, who believed in worker education. They were going to change the world. They did change it."

"So it's not true you've become a pragmatist?"

"It's what people say. I suppose it's true. Partly true. I don't have a political philosophy any more – or only the shreds of one. But you begin to tire of pragmatism."

"When it doesn't work," I said.

He pretended to fall dead. "I told you I wasn't wearing a flak jacket." And then, still smiling: "OK. When it doesn't work."

\*       \*       \*

And yes, out there the Indian summer was persisting – sky still blue, air still still, suburban washing still hanging about in it like clouds, or was it clouds like washing? The dark rough texture of Rangitoto, alight in shades of dark green and black, still made seeing seem like touching, and I tried to see myself as a yacht in the Gulf, with a blue and white spinnaker, leaning to catch a breathless breath; and Dan, unmarried Dan, could be a sloop or a ketch or a yawl, rigged fore and aft but with a gap in the middle still needing to be filled. It was all going on out there, the great daily nothing of the suburb and the weather, the shipping and the tides, the shopping and hedge-trimming and talk of what the Government had and hadn't done, while underground the plates advanced on one another and ground their teeth and checked their watches second by millenial second against the next eruption.

I told Dan about Jacob and he said after Angela and Ben, Jacob should have been Charlie – A, B and C . . .

Speaking of Cs, Dan told me about Caroline – that she was living in Wellington, divorced now, with her two teen-age children, and I said it didn't surprise me Caroline was divorced – only that anyone should have married her in the first place . . .

He said if Jacob had been Charlie, our fourth could have been Dan, A, B, C and D, and I said there would be no fourth . . .

I told him Ginny Scobie was our baby-sitter and he said he found it hard to believe because he could remember when Ros got pregnant and she and Terry decided they would have the baby . . .

He talked nostalgically about the floodlit tennis court where we first met, and my father's rhyme about the One Great Scorer who wrote "not that you won or lost but how you played the game", and I told him Vince – my father – had had a stroke but he was making a good re-covery . . .

I said I didn't play much tennis these days what about him, and he said he played badminton with "our great leader's great deputy" and that it was as well the One Great Scorer didn't record wins and losses because she always beat him . . .

He asked what Ginny Scobie was like and I said not like a Scobie, pretty and bourgeois and a right little fascist. He said that was sad for old Maurice but I told him everyone said Maurice doted on his granddaughter . . .

He told me he'd dreamed of me, just last night, we'd gone out in a dinghy and caught an eel, and I said Oh Dan, not another of your eel dreams . . .

So it went between us, civilized, proper, and these examples must represent the time as it passed above the grinding plates and under the blue and white of windless sky and stalled cloud.

But we did discuss one small matter of business, and it went as follows.

★　　★　　★

He asked about the Mansfield books on my table and I explained that they were really connected with work I was doing on Hilda Tapler – his aunt Amelia. I began to tell him that I was writing a thesis – but he knew. Since his mother's death he was his aunt's nearest surviving relative, and the library let him know of any use that was being made of her papers. He'd intended to talk to me about her cottage. In fact it was one reason ("or an excuse," he said, "if it appeared I needed one") for his visit.

His aunt had left her cottage and the bush section it was built on, which ran all the way down to a little stream, to a writer friend, but the place had been unoccupied since her death, and now the friend had died. The heirs intended to sell it. The cottage would almost certainly be pulled down and the land built on. A group of writers had come to Dan suggesting that it should be bought as some kind of a memorial – not just to Hilda Tapler, who was not a large figure on the literary landscape, but to what she had stood for, and for all the writers of that generation, especially the women. Of course money might be difficult; but there was, Dan said, a bucketful of Lotto profits being splashed around this year. He was looking into it. But because she was his aunt it needed to be clear that he had not himself initiated the idea. He thought if the local community would swing in behind the writers, something might be done.

I told him the North Shore wasn't what it had once been. Commerce ruled. But I was sure at least that people would want the land as a reserve.

I said that Roger was good at community things, and Dan suggested I ask him what might be done. "There'll be

37

a few months before it goes on sale. Probate takes time."

That was all. Perhaps it was the real point of his call, not an excuse, but that for which all the rest – nostalgia, nuances of feeling, echoes from our past – was excuse; but I didn't think so. He had wanted to see me, in fact to give me something. All the time we'd talked it had been lying there in front of him on the coffee table in a large brown official-looking envelope, my name printed across it truculent Dan-bold: "Mrs Laura Barber".

He wasn't able to stay – had asked his driver to be outside at 11.30. We began to say how nice it had been to talk. I told him I watched his career – I think I said "with interest and with pride in his success" – something like that, and he baulked at the word "success".

"Oh, come on now," I said. "You're a Minister of the Crown – the Honourable Dan."

"True. And I quite liked being made the Honourable. But nothing changes, you know. I still get migraines if I drink too much coffee."

It reminded me of some Shakespearean lines, and I quoted them –

> I live with bread like you, feel want,
> Taste grief, need friends. Subjected thus
> How can you say to me I am a king?

He listened, head down, and then looked up, serious. "I'm very susceptible . . ." He didn't say to what.

We were moving towards the door, and now he handed me the envelope. "Would you like to read this? It's something I wrote a few years back – about us. I could never get it right. I wrote a draft and then I kept cutting it down, and cutting it down again – I don't know on what principle. There's not a lot left – probably more than enough."

I took it and slid the typewritten sheets half out. It was headed "The Magic Bagwash", and I read the opening sentence: "It was in the days of euphoria and Dionysus before the new cool."

I'm not sure what I said – thanked him, I suppose, and said I would be glad to read it.

And now at the door he did turn and put his arms around me. I kissed him – once, and then a second time. For just a moment I wished he would do what I was sure he wanted to do – push the door shut again, with us both on the inside – but this was 1990 and the suburbs, and we were two proper people behaving as proper people should.

I think I felt angry as he walked away down the path. He had stirred me up, and now I wouldn't see him again for months, for years, for ever it might as well be.

But I was wrong in that. He would be back – that same day.

# TWO

# 1970 – The Magic Bagwash

It was in the days of euphoria and Dionysus before the
new cool. Protest and pot went around the world
together. Old tough Lyndon Bird was on his way to
becoming a lame duck, and even so many miles away in
Auckland, New Zealand, those of us who had taken our
stand on the sinister side of all the gaps that were being
talked about felt we'd helped. It's not so very long ago,
but already it's as if I'm seeing it through the wrong end
of Aunt April's telescope. I was proprietor of the Anarchist
coffee bar, a place where customers were always
expounding something out of Mailer or Marcuse or Bald-
win or Cleaver or Regis Debray, those voices that seem
from where I stand now as distant as if they came from
the barricades of 1848 or 1789. Bliss was it in that dawn
to be alive, but to be young was absolutely necessary and
it wasn't going to last.

How to describe myself as I was then? Best to begin with
facts: Daniel Cooper, LlB, fourth generation New Zealander, divorced, five feet ten inches, fit and active, slight
build, reddish hair, pale skin, no significant scars or blem-
ishes, sound teeth – but at the age of 27 already passing into
the shadows. My friend Kiev told me once, as she looked
at me with half-closed eyes out of a landscape of crushed
pillows, that I had a determined mouth and she was right.
It was the determination of the timid person, and something
to be reckoned with. In the right war I might have won a
decoration for inconspicuous gallantry. I was a misfit,

sprung from the silent majority to brew coffee for the young warriors of the New Left.

I didn't look much like a protest person. I'd given up the uniform of respectability without putting on all the trappings of the other one. I loved the beautiful people and would have watered their flowers with the last drop out of the desert of my soul, but I think I remained outwardly anonymous. That was why in those days, 1970 and '71, the Auckland police treated me with suspicion – as if I deserved a conviction but they weren't sure for what. I had reason to be grateful to them. They enlarged and sustained the reputation I had among my customers. They went after me at political demonstrations. When they had nothing better to do, a pair would sit in a car outside my flat, watching. Once they searched it for drugs. And two or three times when I had a group performing and some poets reading at the Anarchist they raided it. In these small and relatively painless ways they helped me to appear what I was but couldn't have demonstrated so convincingly otherwise – a misfit, as that great silent money-grubbing cake-eating majority would have said; or as the eloquent minority would have preferred, a radical.

Have we advanced at all? Only a little, I suspect. You know that I had reddish hair and ginger opinions. It hardly amounts to a definition. A man (or so Vince Jackson would have told me) defines himself best in his actions. His doctrines, whatever they may be, are static things, like the features of his face in sleep. In action everything changes from moment to moment. A face may seem to go from youth to age in the course of a few hours' suffering; and a man (this will be my final flourish) who went to bed a sceptic may wake to find himself in love with the world.

★      ★      ★

Our ways of life and of thought were so different, it still surprises me that I should ever have got to know Vince Jackson well enough to have him invite me to his house. He had probably killed his first German while I was still in my mother's womb. He was an importer, a JP, a member of the National Party, an official on sporting bodies – a pillar of society, in fact, the kind of immovable object I was in the habit of rushing against with not quite irresistible force. He became a regular at the Anarchist, but not at all a typical one, and if his first visit had been at a busy hour I'm sure he wouldn't have come back. The long hair, the weird clothes, the beards and beads and sandalled feet, not to mention the opinions, would all have enraged him.

It was quite early in the new year, and he would arrive between 8.30 and 9.00 in the morning to drink a cup of coffee before going to his office. There were no customers at that time of day and I was only there to clean up the mess from the night before. The first time he came in I very nearly turned him away. I came out from the back of the shop and found him already seated, smoking a cigarette, opening his briefcase. He was alone. He looked relaxed. He took out a newspaper, glanced over the front page, lowered it for a moment to watch a young woman passing the window, and returned to it.

Maybe it was that pause while the young woman went by that made me think of him as a fellow being, despite the brutal haircut, the conservative dress, the returned serviceman's badge. Whatever it was, I got him the coffee he asked for. He drank it while he read his paper, paid, and went out. Next day he returned, and the day after.

There was something about him that took hold of my imagination. He seemed to sit in his own enclosure so comfortably I felt a twinge of envy. It wasn't long before we began to exchange a few words about the weather or the news or whatever was going on out in the street. I found him as predictable as, at my first view of him, I'd supposed

42

he would be. If the war in Vietnam was making headlines he would say the Free World had to draw the line somewhere and it was better to fight them there than here. If I mentioned opposition to an All Black tour of South Africa he would tell me it was wrong to mix politics and sport. If there was news of an industrial dispute he talked about "lefties", "wreckers", and "a fair day's work for a fair day's pay". As for the National Government, he thought they were doing "a pretty good job"; but he liked to complain about taxation, the Welfare State, and "bureaucratic controls".

He was like the expensive Swiss watch on his wrist, going round and round in the same grooves as all the other watches – never backwards, never faster or slower, never stopping to reflect. Yet when I asked him something on any of these subjects he would begin by saying "Well, in *my* opinion . . .", or "For what it's worth, *I* believe . . ." It was as if the watch had said, "In my opinion it's 9 o'clock", or "Personally I've come to the conclusion it's 1.30."

I found myself drawing these platitudes from him – and of course they were worthless. But at the same time that I wanted to dismiss Vince along with his ideas, I couldn't help enjoying his confidence and good humour, his aura of wellbeing and of ease with himself.

I sometimes wondered how much or how little he noticed about me. He must have registered my silences. And although none of my regular customers were there at that time of day, he could see the revolutionary posters (Che needs YOU!), the board on which plans and dates for demos, rallies, readings and teach-ins were pinned, the pictures of dope-smoking rock groups. It wasn't, I discovered later, Vince Jackson's habit to hold his fire until he saw the whites of your eyes. But he took it all in and said nothing. Maybe he liked my coffee; or was fascinated to find himself in the enemy camp. Or maybe it was just the weather that kept us from one another's throats.

It was an unusually good summer that had begun before

Christmas and gone on and on. I worked reluctantly, swam when I could, lay awake at night under a sheet listening to the mosquitoes. World events receded. As imagination withered in the sun, so too did sympathy and outrage. When Vince said something enthusiastic about American actions in Vietnam and I didn't respond, I began to feel compromised, as if my political opinions were losing their edge, or were only a luxury to be indulged when the company and the weather made them convenient.

One morning Vince didn't come in at the usual time. The next day I recognized in myself a feeling of anxiety as 8.30 approached, and disappointment when 9 o'clock passed and he hadn't appeared. Next day it was the same. I supposed he must have altered his routine, or found a more congenial place. But on the fourth day he was back.

He told me he'd been spending time down at Stanley Street watching the early rounds of a tennis tournament in which his daughter seemed (as he put it) to be doing rather well for herself.

The Anarchist was in a narrow lane close to Queen Street, and I have a distinct memory of looking hard at Vince Jackson as he told me this, as if I was seeing him for the first time, and then looking beyond him through the glass to the lane. Directly opposite my shop another had been torn down and a new building erected in the narrow gap. I'd taken little interest in this, except to grumble about noise and dust. But now the scaffolding and sacking drapery were gone, and a surprising new façade presented itself, with a series of little blue balconies and white-shuttered windows.

As I peered up at it the thought struck me that my seeing Vince so clearly in that instant, and at the same time noticing the new building, was in some way connected with his having told me he'd spent the past three days watching the tournament. I'd once been a tennis-player myself. For a few years it had been a great passion – part of the middle-class life I'd been brought up in and which I'd only really

44

abandoned after the break-up of my marriage. I'd found it easy enough to leave my job in the Crown Law Office, and to cut myself off from friends and family with whom there had been so many disagreements. Only leaving my tennis club had really bothered me. Tennis had been one thing I knew I'd done well, and enjoyed doing.

I turned my back on the lane and looked again at my customer. "You must be Laura Jackson's father," I said.

"You know something about it then." He was pleased that I'd heard of her.

I told him I'd once played a lot of tennis and that I still followed it. He scolded me for having given it up. He still played himself and he could give the younger ones a run for their money. Even Laura had a healthy respect for his drop shots. He'd laid down a court at home and put in floodlights. In weather like this there was nothing like a game in the cool of the evening to chase away the cobwebs . . .

It was surprising how he rattled on. The tough, wary façade was gone. He seemed younger than his years, and oddly excited. We talked about the tournament and he asked why I hadn't been down to watch. I made the excuse of having to keep the Anarchist running.

Didn't I have assistants? he asked; and when I confirmed that I did, he told me he'd been running his own business since coming back from what he called "Hitler's war", and made a pretty good fist of it. If he regretted anything it was having taken so long to learn that once you had a good staff and the machine was ticking over you could forget about it sometimes and take it easy. In fact your staff worked better if you kept off their backs. If I felt like going to watch the tennis, I should go. What was the use of sweating your guts out to make money if you couldn't take time off now and then to enjoy it?

He was talking to me as a fellow-businessman. That was confusing. So was the fact that it seemed good advice. It was true that for large parts of the day the people I employed didn't need me. What kept me at the Anarchist was the fear that real anarchy might break out – customers might get their lunches free, change might disappear from the till or cartons of cigarettes from the storeroom. All at once this presented itself as the very kind of bourgeois anxiety I thought I'd eliminated.

And what about tennis? Since my private revolution I'd thought of it as a dangerous siren beckoning me back to the rocks of middle-class respectability. Was I now to see it as something that would liberate me from regular hours and the concern for profit?

It was too much to sort out all at once. Our conversation ran on, and when Vince Jackson had gone I was left with the surprising fact that he'd invited me to his house for a game in the evening, and that with scarcely an instant's hesitation, I'd accepted.

*    *    *

It only occurred to me after it had happened how extravagantly (or you might say how crudely, or naively) symbolic it had been to resign from the Crown Law Office to become proprietor of a coffee bar called the Anarchist. But that for a time became my way of life – a series of deliberate actions, mid-course corrections to keep me on target for the moon. When I was a child I used to hear Aunt April say of some young man who had taken up some perfectly obvious occupation that he was "making a life for himself". She said it of me when I qualified in Law and entered the Government service; whereas in fact I was only doing the thing which followed from the thing before in a long chain. It wasn't until the chain was broken that I felt I was exercising free choice. I can't pretend that I became much happier, but at least for the first time I was self-propelled, and there was a certain pride in that.

There's one scene that often comes to mind. I see a small, ginger-haired, pale-skinned child running with flickering feet over orange sand to splash about in the sea. His physique isn't remarkable but his pallor makes him look weaker than he is. He doesn't venture far into the water and after a few minutes dashes back to some wooden steps on which four or five women are sitting. They fuss over him, dry him, rub sun-tan lotion on his back, and hand him a bucket and spade. He begins to dig in the shade of the wooden fence and the pines that grow behind it. Down on the wet sand groups of tanned shouting children are building fortresses with moats the tide will flow into as it advances. The ginger-haired boy who lives in the large house beyond the pines will play in these elaborate diggings when the sun has declined far enough to put them in shadow. By that time the children who made them will have left the beach.

The boy drops his spade and once again runs into the water. In a few minutes he comes out again.

He is myself, of course, and although I seem to observe him from the outside, as if I am one of those anxious women, I recall clearly enough the sensation of passing from sun into shadow – the perceptible coolness of air and sand under the trees, a coolness made sharper and sweeter by the scent of pine gum.

Those women presided over my childhood. Though I had no memory of him, I knew I had a father, but he was rarely spoken of, and I understood that to ask questions about him would distress my mother. I knew that he had gone away to the war and hadn't returned. With my friends I tried to avoid the subject; and when it was unavoidable, to give the impression that it was painful. In that way I was able, without actually being its source, to foster, or anyway do nothing to damage, the myth that my father had been killed on active service – that he had "died for his country". I knew that this wasn't what had happened. He had gone into the army and, rather late in the war, had been sent

47

"overseas". But he had survived unharmed, and had simply failed – neglected, refused (the exact circumstances weren't explained to me) – to come home.

So I was the child of divorced parents at a time when divorce was an embarrassment; but in my case it was something concealed by circumstances. And possibly I didn't press to know more because not to know was a kind of protection. What all this amounts to is that I grew up conscious of being party to a dishonesty – a minor one it now seems, but which at the time gave me a continuing sense of shame.

It must have been late in the war that my mother took me, still a baby, to live in the big family home on the beach left by my grandfather to his daughters, the three As – Averilda, my mother; April, married to a naval officer who was more often at sea than at home; and Amelia, a writer, in fact the author, over the pseudonym Hilda Tapler, of a novel called *Nor Question Much* which was to have, if not a financial triumph, at least for a brief time a *succès d'estime*. Amelia kept a room in the family home but lived a bohemian life in a small cottage several bays to the north.

My mother, my aunts, and their friends looked after me, protected me, and I suppose loved me to excess. It was to please them, or anyway to please my mother and Aunt April, since Aunt Amelia was seldom at home, that I behaved with perfect manners, learned my lessons, embraced opinions which were often unrelated to my inner promptings, and grew up to qualify in Law and to marry Blanche, a girl whom everyone agreed was entirely suitable. No doubt she was. I was the unsuitable one. I'd had no sisters or brothers on whom to practice the arts of war and peace necessary to the state of matrimony; and no mother-and-father to demonstrate them in mature action. When Blanche and I quarrelled I was distressed beyond reason and convinced that she was to blame. When we separated it was as if my own nature was all at once released. I saw that I'd seldom behaved genuinely and sincerely, except that I'd genuinely and sincerely tried to please my minders. Now I had to discover myself, and where there was nothing to discover, invent it. What I discovered first was that I was temperamentally a rebel. I became occasional counsel for the defence of the radical young, and proprietor of the Anarchist.

★　　　★　　　★

That evening I arrived at Vince Jackson's right on 8 o'clock. I walked up the curving gravel drive between beds of roses, the bushes trimmed and standing up straight, tied to props of iron pipe. To these regimented bushes I took an instant dislike, made more acute by the unease I felt at wearing white shirt, shorts, socks and sand shoes. I'd told Vince that I no longer owned a racquet and he'd promised to provide one. But after he'd gone I remembered that tennis was a sport that called for particular gear, and I'd gone out to buy what seemed to be needed. Now I felt as if I'd climbed back into one of the uniforms of my old conforming days.

There was a light on at the entrance and the large front door with its little window of lead-framed glass was ajar. I took hold of the knocker – an iron ring gripped in the teeth of a lion – and rapped. In reply Vince boomed from above, "Come in Danny-boy. I'll be with you in a sec."

I stepped inside on to the soft green carpet that ran everywhere – under double glass doors to the left through which I had an impression of chintz, glass and silver; to the right into a study; straight ahead down a broad, panelled vestibule; and up a stairway that curved away to the left, crossing the vestibule. Light and noise came at me from different parts of the house. I took a further few steps, and as I did Vince appeared on the landing above.

"Oh, you're all dressed up for it," he said.

His shorts and shirt were different shades of brown, the shirt embroidered with his initials, V.E.J.

He led me along the passageway towards the back of the house and we went down a flight of stairs into a broad basement. There, between a table-tennis table at one end and a billiard table at the other, all kinds of sporting gear lay scattered about – skis, surfboards, footballs, masks, bats, footwear, padding.

He was opening a door that slid back on iron rails. "Have a look at the garden," he said.

I walked outside and was assailed by the scent of a trumpet vine. I could hear frogs croaking. The scene didn't at all match those guard-dog roses at the front of the house. The land dropped away in terraces, and against the sky I could see silhouetted heads of tree ferns and cabbage trees. Now Vince switched on the outside lights. They followed a path which zig-zagged down the rock terraces overhung with trees, shrubs, vines and flowers; and at the bottom of the garden I could make out the court, of orange gravel like the path, and flooded with light.

We made our way down, stopping to admire a pool of water lilies, a vine-covered arbour, a bed of flowering shrubs. The resonant croaking of frogs rose and fell, and beyond it, in a different pitch and key, that faint but constant gabble from the house.

I'd mentioned to Vince that it was a long time since I last played tennis and that he mustn't expect too much of me; and now, as we walked on to the court, I began to say it all again.

"Don't let's have any excuses," he said, "or I might have to compare our ages."

And then, still smiling, he quoted

> For when the One Great Scorer comes
> To write against your name,
> He marks – not that you won or lost
> But how you played the game.

It sounded like something Aunt April might have quoted and I didn't know whether I was supposed to laugh or look pious so I mumbled something inaudible and made a few swings with my racquet.

We began with a practice knock. When it had gone on long enough he came up to the net and suggested we start. I noticed that he wasn't breathing hard, as I was. He told me I didn't need any excuses – I had every stroke in the book. I didn't deny it. It had never been the strokes I'd lacked, only the temperament.

We played two sets and Vince won them both. Anything he'd lost in strength and aggressiveness over the years he'd obviously made up in stamina, steadiness and cunning. I wasn't disappointed with my game. I'd enjoyed it. I felt that liberation peculiar to controlled physical effort. It seemed a good start. But I'd no sooner thought this, and said it, than I had to ask myself, a start to what? And then I remembered that in the course of a long rally involving net rushes, lobs and retreats to the back line, the thought of the Anarchist, with its endless exploratory talk, had entered some neutral, disengaged part of my consciousness and at that moment it had seemed remote, alien. Recalling this as we came off the court I was puzzled. How could the pursuit of truth have seemed, even for a moment, less humanly creditable than the pursuit of a ball?

Vince was unwinding a lanyard from a bracket fixed to the trunk of a tree and in a moment he was letting it out hand over hand. I looked up expecting, I suppose, a flag. Descending from an out-flung bough was a large dome, like an enormous bird-cage, its framework wire and thin steel, its covering transparent gauze. Vince explained that it "kept the mozzies out". They were a nuisance at this time of year. "Don't bother you while you're on the move but the moment you sit down they're in like Flynn."

The dome settled over a table and chairs on which he'd set out bottles of beer and glasses. He held the flap open and we stepped inside. Once we were seated everything appeared as before, except that the gauze around us caught the light and glowed faintly.

We hadn't been there long when Laura appeared. She must have come down by another path. A sound caught my attention and there she was at the far end of the court, swinging her racquet, loosening up. Vince called to her and she said she would be over in a minute. There was a knot she had to untie in her service.

She took up her position and began – a strong fast service straight down the centre line, followed by a slower, high-kicking one to the outside. She picked up another pair of balls and repeated the service from the left court; then a further pair from the right. When there were none left she walked slowly to the other end of the court, gathered them together, and repeated it all. Every ball seemed to go pretty much where it was meant to. But it was the ritual quality that impressed me. I imagined these same movements without the racquet and ball – her left arm thrown up, her hand opening to the heavens, the right arm striking violently, the torso collapsing forward, and then the slow, measured walk down the court to where those gestures, at once graceful and passionate, were repeated. She was like the priestess of a mystery. It's hardly too much to say that I was already in love with her.

Her movements up and down the court had the deliberateness of someone conscious of being watched; but I felt certain they would have been exactly the same if we hadn't been there. She would always act *as if* she were being watched. Or maybe she was watching herself. The pace seemed a fraction slower than would have been natural to her, and the length of the stride a fraction longer. Her head was very steady on her shoulders and there was something of an effort in the movements, as if she'd been wading in shallow water or thrusting through long grass. She didn't appear tightly reined in, but to have imposed certain restraints on herself in the interests of a style which, it seemed to me, was something more than just the style of a tennis player.

When she'd finished her practice she gathered up her gear and came over to join us. Vince pushed back the flap and she stepped into the cage, saying she thought she'd worked out what had gone wrong.

Vince introduced us. I shook her hand and the three of us sat down and talked about the tournament. She seemed to me the most desirable young woman I had ever encountered. I felt as if I was floating in space, and I couldn't take my eyes off her.

Our talk wandered away from tennis. Vince mentioned the Anarchist, and Laura, smiling, said, "That's the Make-Love-Not-War place."

"Make Love Not War," Vince repeated. "Why not both?" And then, perhaps because neither of us responded, he began to tell us a story out of his own war experience. He'd been with the New Zealand Division in Italy. His unit had been cut off and was being strafed by German fighter planes. They'd withdrawn into a wood but planes were still overhead, attacking. The men were hungry. They'd been trying to get to an abandoned cottage in which one of them a few days before had seen boxes of tinned food. There was an open space between the wood and the cottage with only single trees here and there. Vince judged the downward sweeps of the planes and made his dash between them to the nearest tree in the open. As the next plane came down he moved around the trunk keeping it between him and the guns. He saw the leaves of the tree flickering as bullets went through, saw the dust spurting up on either side, felt the impact of bullets striking the tree on the other side, and at that moment he made his run to the next tree – and so on until he reached the cottage.

"I burst in," Vince said, "still holding my rifle – and what did I find? One lost Jerry officer with a pistol pointing straight at me. I thought, This is bad. Not, I've had it – just This is bad. And then I saw the pistol was wobbling all over the place. The poor bugger was shaking like a leaf."

He seemed to retreat inside the story, as if it was finished. "What did you do?" I asked, but he didn't hear – or anyway he didn't reply.

I envied him – and then struggled against that feeling. What was the use of experiences like that if they left you as predictable as a Swiss watch, mouthing the thoughts and opinions served up by a sheet of newsprint? No experience was denied an active imagination. And on the other hand without imagination you might experience every kind of human action and be left unaffected. I told myself this; but for just that moment I wasn't sure I believed it.

"I've still got that pistol in my room," he said.

I felt myself flinch. I looked at Laura – in fact I'd half watched her all the time he'd been telling his story. Maybe I'd hoped she would appear bored, or better still disgusted. But I could detect nothing. While Vince had spoken she'd appeared to be listening, but not with special attention; to be detached and yet not disapproving. Her façade was perfect, impenetrable, and when Vince had said that he still had the pistol, I was the one who reacted with shock. It jolted me because I'd so clearly imagined the German officer's fear, and now I was sure Vince must have killed him.

He stood up, stretching. "Enough for one night," he said, and stepped through the flap. "Hold on to your hats." He hauled on the lanyard so the cage rose into the trees. For just a moment Laura and I sat smiling at one another.

"I'll take the racquets up," Vince said. "Lower the net, will you, Laura?"

I began to follow him, then turned back to see if she needed help. She was at the net-post, turning a long handle. It creaked, and the frogs croaked in reply from the pond. She paused at the gate and looked up into the trees. Then she came up the path towards me. When she reached me she had to stop. We stood facing one another. My mind was blank. I was as surprised as she must have been when I heard myself speaking in a quiet, precise voice. Even now I'm not quite sure what I said. It was something brief, and too intimate, if not in the words chosen then certainly in the tone. It still embarrasses me to think of it – all my ginger-haired freckled intensity laid open before her.

At that moment Vince must have reached the basement because some of the lights went out. I was glad of that, but still I didn't have the wit to stand aside and let her pass.

It was she who moved first. She reached out in the semi-darkness and put her hand over mine. "Come on," she said. "He'll be getting impatient up there." I turned my hand over to grasp hers but in a moment she'd detached herself. We walked in silence on up the path.

$$\star \qquad \star \qquad \star$$

Aunt April occupied the best room in the house. Its windows couldn't be seen from the beach but they looked past the pines and beyond the wooden fence to the Hauraki Gulf and the island of Rangitoto. There was a telescope at one of the windows. My uncle Bert, the naval officer who rose to the rank of commander, had given it to his wife so that she could watch his ship come and go. I don't remember seeing her use it, but it provided my favourite game whenever I was allowed into her room.

After I met Laura Jackson an idea came to me which was new and almost certainly unfounded, but which seemed so right and so satisfying I wasn't quite able to rid myself of it. It was that my aunt, who seldom bothered to watch her husband's ship, had watched my father's, when he left to go abroad, from the moment it entered the Gulf until it disappeared over the horizon. In my mind I saw her following the ship as it sailed past Rangitoto, taking her eye from the glass only to wipe away a tear that blurred her vision. I saw this comic-strip vision as if it had been a real memory, but I knew it couldn't be. It was true that Aunt April's few references to my father had always been less chilly than my mother's. She made it clear that he had been in the wrong; but her condemnation lacked bitterness. She would say, "Your father, Dan? Brett was a charming man, clever, but irresponsible I'm afraid." And I used to imagine (perhaps because it was what I wanted to believe) that her eyes and her tone of voice were hinting that she might herself have found Brett Cooper preferable to the naval commander who, for all his braid and whiskers, hadn't succeeded in giving her any children.

But if an affair between my father and my aunt had helped to break up my parents' marriage, was it likely the two sisters would have lived comfortably together afterwards? And since I had been born after my father's departure overseas, how could I possibly have seen my aunt watching his ship sail out?

Still the image remained stubbornly in my mind. I recalled having seen a photograph of my aunt as a young woman dressed in white and carrying a tennis racquet, and now I wondered whether it was fanciful to think she'd looked remarkably like Laura Jackson. Then I would see my father as a young Vince Jackson and wonder whether it wasn't some dim sense of a family resemblance that had first drawn me to Vince.

\*      \*      \*

The euphoria of that first encounter with Laura couldn't last but it was very potent. When I left the Jackson house that evening I drove here and there about the town, uncertain where I was or what I wanted to do next. I found myself on the Waterfront Drive, I stopped at Mission Bay and watched coloured lights changing in the fountain, I returned to their house and parked under plane trees outside, staring up at the windows which were now all in darkness. Everything seemed sharply defined, brilliant, beautiful. It was that kind of a night, but I don't doubt it would have looked the same to me in any weather.

It wasn't until next morning that I began to worry. I'd had a dream which began well but turned into a nightmare. I was walking up and down a beach at the edge of the water with Laura. The sun was shining and waves broke and shot forward covering our feet with white foam. And then the foam cleared as the water surged further forward over the sand, and we could see small fish skimming over shells and around our ankles. We were both carrying tennis racquets and we walked on, loftily it seemed, through the shallows. This went on for a long time. But a pile of corpses, mutilated and decaying, appeared on the beach. Each had a numbered tag. A man came up and told me that two of the corpses were mine. He seemed to be congratulating me, as if I'd got them at a bargain price. I tried to get away from him, saying I couldn't take them just now, but he insisted. And then I was driving my car. Laura was beside me. I didn't look behind but I knew that upright in the back seat were the two corpses with their tags.

That morning as I went mechanically through the business of showering, shaving, making breakfast, I was filled with anxiety. Wasn't Laura Jackson only the entirely suitable girl in a new and brighter package? Didn't my association with her family threaten the new life I'd constructed out of the ruins of the old? I was convinced that I ought to have nothing more to do with her. But I didn't trust myself. Vince would come back to the Anarchist. He would invite me to his house. I would go there again and fall under their spell.

I didn't know how to interpret Laura's response to what I'd said to her on the path. For a moment it had seemed almost an expression of complicity. But more likely it had been only a cool and efficient way of dealing with an awkward encounter. She might have liked my directness; equally she might have found it distasteful, and taken my hand only to pacify me while she got past.

I decided action was called for. But what kind? I sat in a chair and tried to think to some purpose. Thinking was made difficult by the noise of cicadas. I'd never heard them so raucous. They began before the birds, even before the crickets were silent, and continued all day, until the very last of the light was gone. It was only a minor irritation, but it added to my confusion.

My flat overlooked trees on the upper slopes of Grafton Gully. Further down, bulldozers were working, tearing out vegetation to prepare for a new motorway. Clouds of dust rose up and hovered in the early morning light. The cicadas crackled and buzzed. I became conscious of an item of news broadcast on my radio. It caught my attention and helped me towards an idea – a plan of action.

An American official, one of the President's closest advisers, was due that afternoon in Auckland. He was a sort of travelling salesman with the Vietnam war in his briefcase, and he was here to discuss with the Prime Minister a further contribution of New Zealand troops. A big demonstration was planned outside his hotel and I'd intended being there, first shutting the Anarchist with a sign "Closed for the Demo". Now I thought I might take a more active part. I would try to do something unacceptable, get myself arrested, and let the Jacksons know about it, so that even if my resolve to steer clear of them weakened, they wouldn't want me back.

It wasn't much of a plan but it was all I could think of, and after all, in those times of social discord, it might have worked. At least it settled my mind for the time being.

There's no need to say much about the events of that day. One demonstration is pretty much like another. They're good sport if you have a streak of the anarchist in you, but not everyone has. This was, as my customers were saying next day, a good one – by which was meant that the newspapers, the police, the Government, even the Opposition, were outraged, or pretended to be. For me, however, it was a failure.

It was soon obvious that I wasn't going to get close to the distinguished visitor. Then I had the idea that I would throw at him an apple which I happened to have in the pocket of my jacket. It wouldn't be a very glorious or dramatic gesture, but it should be enough to get me arrested and possibly get my name into the papers.

But the visitor was late arriving and in the meantime, waiting to do my bit or my thing – to go over the top, as Vince Jackson might have said – I couldn't keep still. I yawned, my hands prickled, I chattered to the people on either side of me. In the end, without thinking, I began to eat the apple. Long before the official party arrived it was gone. After that I did my best. I pushed and heaved and shouted. I was in the thick of it all. But I'd failed to get anywhere near the front or to catch the eye of the one or two policemen who might have been glad of an excuse to arrest me.

Back at my flat that evening I turned on the television to watch the local news. I was too late. Instead of seeing the demonstration I saw the last few points of the match in which Laura Jackson had beaten the top-seeded player. She was into the final.

When Vince came into the Anarchist in the morning he couldn't conceal his excitement. "She's done bloody well," he said. "It doesn't matter whether she wins or not." Maybe he was thinking of the One Great Scorer; but it was obvious that whether she won or lost mattered a great deal.

He asked was I going to watch the final. Without having thought about it, I answered at once that I was.

"Good man," he said. "Then you'd better have a decent seat." And he handed me a ticket.

Laura won her match that day. I don't think I'd ever doubted that she would. She played with great concentration, looking at no one, speaking to no one, cut off from her opponent, from the crowd, from the umpire and ball boys, walking about the court between rallies with that deliberate slow stride of hers. Twice when the umpire called a doubtful fault on her first service she walked slowly to the back of the court, touched the wooden railing with her racquet, and returned to deliver the second. That was the furthest extent to which she showed any emotion.

The seat Vince had got for me was low in the stand and close to the centre of the court. Each time the players changed ends they passed close to me, pausing to mop their faces with towels and to take drinks. Once only Laura turned towards the stand while she held a towel around the lower part of her face, pressing it with both hands against her ears and the back of her neck. For a few seconds her eyes were directed straight at mine and I thought almost certainly she had seen me, but she turned away, showing neither interest nor indifference – showing nothing at all.

When the match was over I left the stand at once. For more than an hour I waited at the entrance, hoping to catch sight of her as she came out. I wanted to congratulate her, and to let her know I'd seen her win. There was no shade. The sun struck up from the pavement and off the concrete block wall enclosing the grounds. As time passed I felt dizzy. Zigzag lines of migraine cut across my vision and when my eyes cleared my head ached. People were coming and going through the gates and at times it was difficult to be sure I'd seen them all, but I clung to my post.

It was the sound of her voice that attracted my attention. I turned and saw her standing at the edge of the pavement clutching her racquets under one arm, saying goodbye to someone, then waving and calling into the traffic. A white sports car drew up and she got in, dropping her racquets into the gap behind the seats and pushing back the hair

60

from her face. I recognized the driver. His name was Roger Barber and his father was a judge known to the protest movement for a ruling on "disorderly behaviour" which all subsequent cases referred to.

I hurried forward as the car began to move, and then stopped. "Oh Dan," she said. "Hullo." And she flashed me a lovely smile.

"Congratulations," I shouted. "You were beautiful."

She shouted her thanks, and waved to me as the car pulled noisily away.

"You were beautiful. You are beautiful," I said to the back of her head as it disappeared up the street.

I walked unsteadily through the crowd around the gates, reached the grass at the edge of the Domain Drive, and sat down in the shade of a tree. There was a great deal of movement and noise, and my head still ached. Then, out of the confusion of sleek cars and neatly-dressed people something familiar appeared. It was a big, old-style Ford driven by the town's most colourful young radical, Terry Scobie. Its doors were painted in swirling purples and reds. There were four others and a dog inside and I had an impression of hair, teeth, and floral cloth, all in great quantities.

I staggered to my feet, waving. The Ford rattled up on to the grass verge and I was dragged into the back seat like a man being rescued from the sea.

"Poor Dan," a girl said. "Was it a bad trip?"

Her name was Kiev. I stood up as the car began to move, and fell back beside her. The dog, known as Ho, licked my ear.

Kiev took my hand and thrust it down between her thighs as if to anchor me. We pulled away through the crowds. In the front seat a man called Justin Pope was making what looked like the sign of the cross over their heads. "Bless you, brothers and sisters," he shouted. "Bless you, you sweet fuckers."

On the other side of Kiev a couple called Janet and John

61

were scattering leaflets. We followed the traffic up the road that wound through trees into the Domain, passed below the Cenotaph and the white columns of the Museum, turned left into the main road, and began winding down into the lower reaches of Parnell. At my feet were half a dozen cartons of Chinese food. I was hungry. I was glad to be rescued, and depressed that I should have felt I needed to be.

*    *    *

Two days later I was still at their house in Parnell. Let me give you the scene. It's evening. The last of the sunlight is coming through french doors open to a garden overgrown with weeds, heavy with the scent of flowers and citrus trees. I'm sitting on an apple box in the doorway holding up, to catch the last of the light, a notebook from which I'm reading aloud. My subject is the war in Vietnam. The five people who were in the Ford are listening. The dog, Ho, is there too, sleeping on his side on cracked brown linoleum which at its edges shows faint traces of its original pattern of squares and intersecting triangles. On the floor, almost at my feet, is the owner of the Ford, Terry Scobie. He is one of those warriors of the New Left, long and lean, good-looking, Zapata-moustached, beaded, jeaned, sandalled, with long black hair held back from his face by a head-band. Sitting back-to-back with him is his friend, Ros, his fierce female replica. Ros is pregnant, and now and then Terry reaches around to put a hand on her belly, feeling for the kicks from within which she has begun to report in recent days. Janet and John, the couple whose house it is, are lying top-and-tail on an old couch.

Justin Pope – "the Pope" as he's sometimes called – is on another apple box. While I read he stares at the ceiling, slowly scratching his scalp. Somewhat older than the others, he has the look of an Old Testament prophet. His feet are bare. His beard and hair are uncut and unkempt. His trousers are flannel bags that might almost date from the 1930s. His shirt is purple and covered in small red flowers, and over it he wears a leather jerkin.

Finally there's Kiev. She's deep in the only comfortable chair, sewing. She's one of those young women who give the impression (is it something to do with the way they dress?) of being shapeless – neither fat nor thin; but with a beautiful, peaceful face, and delicate pale hands. She has blue eyes, unchangingly passive and solemn, like the eyes of a Madonna. From time to time she looks up, and when she does there's neither appeal nor animation nor, on the other hand, vacancy. It's like being covered in velvet or enclosed in the wings of an enormous moth. The rest of her face composes itself around the eyes in which all the life is concentrated. Her stillness is appropriate to the scene but it would probably be the same if a funny conversation, a violent quarrel, or an orgy were raging around her. She's always like that – passive, amenable, available, imperturbable – and because I've been sharing her bed these past nights I direct my reading especially to her.

But it's Terry who is listening most eagerly. He has also taken out the dope bag, rolled a smoke, and is now holding a deep lungful while he passes it on. I know that for him this is only to enhance the pleasure. From Terry the smoke comes as a kind of acclamation.

So much for the scene. Now for the explanation. How have I reached this point? That's more difficult.

After I'd spent my first evening at the house I decided that for the time being I wanted to stay, and I made arrangements for the Anarchist to be looked after while I took a few days off. Maybe I was afraid to leave. I felt protected there. The Jacksons weren't going to come knocking at the door of this leper colony and lead me away. But my friends all had things to do during the day. Janet and John ran a shop in which they sold Indian and African goods –

jewellery, sandals, belts, ornaments, rugs and screens. Terry was on bail on a charge of obstruction, and obliged to report daily at the Central police station, after which he worked as a clerk for one of the trade unions. Ros was an assistant at the Anarchist. Justin Pope was a self-appointed social worker. He described himself as a Buddhist-Catholic. He had once been (or so he liked to say) an alcoholic, and now he devoted himself to the care of alcoholics and drug addicts. And Kiev – three days a week she worked at the Anarchist; and on the others I didn't know where she went. I knew nothing about her relations with other men; and because it might have suggested a possessiveness I didn't feel and which wouldn't have been welcome, I didn't ask.

That left only the dog, Ho, a big friendly mongrel whose doggy smell I didn't find offensive and whose companionship I enjoyed.

I had to have something to do, and I thought I would try writing – something topical, political, reflective. Justin gave me some school notebooks and I applied myself, writing first about American foreign policy since the Second World War, trying to simplify what I knew, sort it into order and sequence, and give it a backbone of opinion, keeping the war in Vietnam always in mind as its logical outcome.

But I must explain that there was something about this exercise which troubled me right from the start. I couldn't conceal from myself that although she was never mentioned, my essay was addressed to Laura Jackson. Her image presided over the table at which I worked. It was no use telling myself that she was irrelevant. She was there and I couldn't be rid of her. It was as if I were writing her a love-letter, a bitter one, full of recriminations, saying in effect, "You want to pretend that this war is not your responsibility, but tennis won't save you. Vietnam belongs to us all."

On the third day I wrote about some of the worst brutalities of the war. I think it was before the My Lai massacre had become public knowledge. But those of us who read the protest literature knew already of similar events, and it seemed to me that some of these had to be isolated and described; because my argument was that the war was a true expression of American foreign policy, and that the atrocities were a true expression of the war.

So I come back to the scene I've described and to myself sitting on an apple box delivering my harsh sentences in a plain, tough tone, seeing Terry Scobie clench his fist and drive it against a floor board.

Terry's conversation had lately taken on a desperate quality. He'd had enough of the moderate protest movement, which he said had become established, accepted, almost comfortable, and was taken as a sign that "democracy was working". It was serving a bourgeois purpose and could achieve nothing but the release of individual feelings. What was needed, he argued, was dramatic action.

When I'd finished reading that evening Terry was more emphatic than ever. Violence, explosives, blood – they were inevitable; they were necessary.

"You mean other people's blood," Justin said.

"Whose do you suggest?" Terry was indignant. "Our own?"

But Justin didn't rule that out. "Martyr's blood," he said. "Someone with a gallon of gas and a match on the steps of the Museum – it might take the protest movement a long way. The monks have done it in Vietnam."

"That's your thing, not mine," Terry said. "You're the Buddhist." It was difficult to know when Justin was being serious. Now he closed his eyes and his head went back as if he was in communication with some higher power, reporting on what was coming to him. In a voice like Marlon Brando's he intoned, "'Lord.' I say, 'just give me the word.' 'Love,' he says. 'Love is the word.' I say, 'Lord, this injustice is too great to be borne.' 'I bear it,' he says."

"Are you sure it's Him?" Kiev asked.

Next day when they went off in the car I found I had a problem. I read over what I'd written and for a long time I couldn't see where I was to go next. But it didn't seem to me I'd finished. Laura's image remained. It stared at me, unsatisfied. "Go on," it said. "What follows from all this?"

I'd closed my account of the Vietnam war with some of its worst atrocities. This led me to think about human suffering in general, and once I'd given my mind to that I was so weighed down I had to begin writing again just to get above it. The obvious examples came first – the extermination of the Jews, the Stalinist purges, Hiroshima, the Dresden fire-bombing. We thought of these as peculiar to our age, but only the technology was new. Out of even a rudimentary knowledge of history there marched a succession of horrible images – crucifixions, burnings, massacres, tortures. Each example was like a small separate ineradicable scar on my consciousness marking the moment at which the knowledge had been first acquired. Only now I brought them all together and added them to my view of Vietnam. It wasn't that they mitigated the present-day horror or lessened the guilt. But they gave horror and guilt a larger context. Cruel slaughter wasn't a norm of human societies, but in one form or another it was something like a constant.

So I passed from history to a philosophical meditation which led in turn to a kind of mysticism. Having written myself into a state of commitment to action I wrote myself slowly but surely out of it. Terry's explosives were defused. I passed through the spectrum of the protest movement's doctrines, from Western radicalism to Eastern quietism, and finished up contemplating my navel among the citrus trees. Couldn't one love God – even a God in whom one didn't believe – by playing tennis? Could one, on the other hand, love Him by doing harm even to the worst of His creatures? My love letter, which had begun with recriminations, ended by taking them all back. Laura Jackson had never been

66

mentioned but she'd been present all the time, and her image was left glitteringly intact.

On the evening of my final reading Terry walked out into the garden before I'd finished, followed a minute later by Ros. I read the last page and closed my notebook.

Janet shook her head. "You're not practical, Dan."

"He's not trying to be practical," Justin said. "He's trying to think."

"How does it help a Vietnamese peasant," John asked, "to know that Dan's thinking?"

"How does anything help?" Kiev asked. "Dan's getting on with life in his own way. That's what we're all doing, isn't it?"

"Some ways are more useful than others," Janet insisted.

Terry and Ros came back from the garden. Terry was frowning. I knew it was time for me to go.

Soon I had gathered up my things and said my thanks and farewells. Justin said he would walk some of the way with me. I called goodbye to Terry and Ros who had disappeared into a bedroom but there was no reply – only a violent bumping from their bed, which I hoped would do no harm to Ros's passenger. I put my hand on Kiev's cheek and she pulled me down to kiss her goodbye. Janet and John came to the gate with her to see me off.

Justin and I walked up to the ridge, past the White Heron motel, and down the steps to Judge's Bay. It was late, the tide was full, there was no one about, and on an impulse we stripped and made our way gingerly into the cool water. Justin wasn't much of a swimmer but he managed to make it all the way to the railway embankment, alternating breast-stroke and a kind of dog-paddle. There we sat while he got his breath back.

"Terry's not pleased with me," I said.

"Never mind," he said. "You don't need him to be, do you?"

His wet face shone a bronzy colour in the lights from the

Waterfront Drive, and I wondered was he Maori or just dark Celt. The question had come up before and he'd insisted that "Maori" and "Pakeha", "English" and "Celt", were definitions he rejected now that he was a Buddhist. So was "New Zealander". "I went to India," he'd explained, "and there I learned that I was part of a big rough family called the human race."

"Cold here, man," he said now, hugging himself and slapping his upper arms.

We slid into the water and made our way back. We dressed and I said goodbye to him and walked up the slope towards the Rose Gardens. I felt my pace accelerating, as if I'd been away a long time and was anxious to get home.

*   *   *

I look over the final sentences in the notebooks I carried back that night from the house in Parnell: "In the fifties the cry of the young who had no war to fight and no revolution to accomplish was 'Give us a cause'. Now we believe we have one. We would like to say, like the patriots of heroic ages, 'Give us Honour or give us Death', but we know in our hearts that in the sphere of public affairs we will be denied them both. Our weapons are newsprint and wasted breath, our victories and defeats a matter of individual calculus. There are no bodies to be counted, no territory won or lost, no ecstasy but that of the hemp and the poppy, no anguish but that of waking from our dream of action to find ourselves still talking."

It's not surprising that Terry hadn't waited to hear the end, and not surprising either that I was at the Anarchist early next morning looking out for Vince Jackson. He turned up right on time. A day or so later he invited me for another game of tennis at his house. That evening we took a set each while Laura sat watching under the mosquito-net cage.

Soon I was seeing a lot of the Jacksons. I thought Laura was in two minds about me, so for a time I took things slowly. It wasn't as difficult as I might have expected. I don't mean that I found her less mysterious and attractive – only that I was content for the moment to stand off from her, to watch her, to relish the sense of being quietly and peacefully in love with her, as one might be in love with an idea.

But she couldn't remain an idea. She had to become a person, and did; and the person who replaced the idea, without destroying for me its still shimmering presence, was not quite as I'd imagined her. Inside the young woman who had seemed committed only to tennis there was another looking for escape from her family and the kind of success it expected of her, and who perhaps saw in me, not a person uncertain like herself and wanting definition, but the rebel, the man of action, owner of the Anarchist, counsel for the defence of the radical young. It was as if our paths had crossed because for the moment we were moving in opposite directions.

The summer was coming to an end. For ten days it rained. Tennis wasn't possible. I had no excuse for visiting the Jacksons, but I went without one and was welcomed.

The rain passed but now it was a late-summer sun. The days were shorter – beautiful, fresh, clear, no longer humid. Ginger plant flowered in the gully below my flat. Plumes of toi-toi stood out against the sky shaken by sparrows which clung, fluttering, raiding the seeds. The harbour like the sky was blue. There were fresh apples. Everything looked good and tasted good.

My instinct was to remain still, not to advance on Laura at all but wait until the right moment presented itself. But I felt anxious. Suppose I waited too long and the whole thing dissolved into nothing? Or suppose it was just something going on in my head? I knew that Roger Barber, the young man who had picked her up that day outside the

Stanley Street courts, was still about with his white sports car, getting no encouragement but waiting for his chance.

I was looking for a sign, a signal that might never come. I'd recently begun sending linen from the Anarchist to a laundry. It was called the Magic Bagwash and its motto was "Everything Comes Out White". Each week a bag was collected and a bag returned but I was never sent an account. I mentioned this to the delivery man and he said, obviously knowing little and caring less about such things, that he was sure one would come. I decided that when I got an account from the Magic Bagwash I would make my move. That would be my signal. I wasn't sure what I would do, but in the meantime I would wait.

All this time I'd found my mind turning often to thoughts of my family. One night I left the Anarchist late and instead of going home I drove across the Harbour Bridge. There was a moon trailing across the flat waters of Big Shoal Bay and it travelled with me towards Takapuna. When I got to the beach where my mother and aunt lived I parked the car and walked along the sand. The Gulf was calm and I could make out Rangitoto under the moon. There was no light in the big house beyond the paling fence. Next day I rang my mother to ask whether any photograph of my father had survived. She said when I paid them a visit she would see if she could find one for me.

So I went home for the first time in many months. It was April, my birthday month, and they had presents for me. There was a certain amount of quiet grumbling at my prolonged absence but it passed. I roamed about the house, swam – though the water was cold now – and walked along the beach. I watched ships through my aunt's telescope, and stayed for a meal, for which I had brought the wine. We were well into our second bottle when I looked across the table at the two sisters and asked why they never talked about my father. It felt such a bold and unacceptable question I was surprised when it didn't provoke a flurry of protest and resentment. But it did produce what seemed to me evasion.

"What's there to say?" my mother asked. "It's so long ago. Brett went away to the war and he chose not to come back. That war did strange things to our men."

"And you don't know where he is?"

"I don't want to know," she said, which didn't seem quite to answer my question.

But she did give me a photograph of the two of them, a young couple in tennis gear, holding their racquets, on the court which had once been beside the house. My father wasn't in the least like Vince Jackson. He was like me. But hadn't my mother been the same physical type as Laura? Weren't their eyes, and the set of the head, alike? I thought so anyway.

Two days later, on my birthday, my account came from the Magic Bagwash.

\*       \*       \*

I have spent a lot of time writing this fragment of autobiography – for what purpose I'm not sure. There are many ways it might be brought to a conclusion, each different, each perfectly truthful. Here is just one.

It's a year or so after the events already described and I'm lying on sand under a pohutukawa. A small sand hill hides the sea from view, but I can hear it rolling in and breaking not far away. I'm tired from a long walk, down a difficult West Coast valley, taken with a group of friends led by Terry Scobie's father, Maurice. For the moment Laura and I are separated from the group but we will soon join up again and spend the night in a bach in a hollow called (if the sign there is to be believed) Happy Valley. A breeze is blowing offshore – unusual on this coast, but not unknown. To my left, bronze flax fronds, split lengthwise by the winds, make a faint clatter as they move. Above me long boughs of pohutukawa spread horizontally across the sky. Through these boughs and their clusters of leaf I can see puffs of white cloud lingering and drifting. Further down the sky the cloud is banking.

I ask myself why I ever chose to assume the persona of the committed rebel, and felt obliged to live up to it. Then I wonder whether the question represents laziness, or exhaustion – or could it be simply truthful self-recognition?

The boughs scarcely move in the breeze up there against a benign sky. I can hear Laura coming over dry sand that squeaks underfoot. Behind closed eyes I imagine driftwood and smooth stones. I want this moment to stretch out into eternity. It's my notion – the only one I have – of heaven. "Everything comes out white." Haven't we, Laura and I, at least for this moment on warm sand and in sound of the sea, tilted the balance of forces in our universe a little towards the good?

# THREE

## 1971-2 – The Other Coast

Soon after Dan got his account from the Magic Bagwash Laura left home and moved into a flat in Grafton with Caroline. From Dan's flat to theirs was only five minutes' walk.

That same year the Anarchist was closed, the building that housed it scheduled for demolition, and Dan took over managing a bookshop in High Street. The group that had gathered at the Anarchist met now at another bookshop, Lefty's. Dan seldom went there, but his obsession with Vietnam continued. Laura remembers the Tet Offensive, the bombing of North Vietnam, the Paris peace talks which never seemed to get beyond arguments about what shape the table was to be and who should sit at it, the invasion of Cambodia, Watergate . . . All of that became part of her life because it was part of Dan's, but never quite as close to the centre as it was for him.

Sitting at the big table, Tapler papers and Mansfield books spread out, morning light glinting off the sea through a shower blowing down the Gulf like a fine net of silver or a scarf of transparent silk, she thinks of what Dan has written and tries to sink right back inside herself, back into her memories of that time; and what comes most vividly is not politics at all, but the atmosphere of old rooms and an overgrown garden, a chipped bath, a cracked handbasin, painted wooden kitchen cupboards with small wobbly handles, wallpapers with flower patterns mercifully faded, a faint smell of gas from a leaking stove, tendrils and vine leaves creeping in through gaps and open windows, and Leonard Cohen singing about a half-mad woman called Susannah, a song with the refrain "and you love her perfect body with your mind" – the "perfect body" of those years being seen more often horizontal than upright on the tennis court.

But her other vivid image of that time is of West Auckland – the Waitakeres, the Scenic Drive, the bush and black sand beaches of the coast north of the Manukau Harbour. They had friends there and drove out almost every weekend, and sometimes two or three evenings during the week, most often to a rambling house occupied by an American couple, Dick and Lee Lomas and their children Richard and Rosie. Dick Lomas was a scientist with the DSIR, an expert on water pollution. They had left America because of the war in Vietnam, and also because New Zealand was, Dick said (giving the word that American pronunciation which puts the emphasis not on the first syllable but on the second) "the last frontier". They were Californians, used to luxury – Dick from a business family in San Francisco, Lee the daughter of a famous maker of B-grade movies – and they entered into the life of what must have seemed to them Third World poverty in a spirit of adventure, taking pleasure in living in a wooden house which didn't keep out the winter draughts, and driving a big old car referred to always as the Wreck. To everyone who knew them they seemed a marvellous couple, she beautiful and clever, he subtle, slow-spoken, powerful . . .

The silver scarf of rain has passed over Rangitoto and for a moment the sky is mostly clear and the sea a patchwork of blue and deeper blue. Laura closes her eyes and lets her mind rove over that image of the house high up in the bush of the Waitakeres, the lazy, soothing American voices, the click of table-tennis bat on ball, the rustle of wind through leaves as they sat drinking on the verandah, the sound of cars on the road below . . .

*     *     *

74

Was it a path, or a narrow road, that wound up above and behind the Lomases' house? We walked up there sometimes in the daytime, but more often at night. From the hilltop you could see the whole of Auckland city, the whole width of the peninsula from one harbour to the other. On a clear night the lights were like stars. Once I walked up there with Maurice Scobie. Or maybe we all went, but Dan returned with Lee and Dick leaving Maurice and me alone on the hill. Maurice was a lot older than the rest of us. As a youth he'd fought in the International Brigades in the last year of the Spanish Civil War. He'd been a Communist, a Party member; and after he'd fought in Spain his faith had been shaken by news of Hitler's pact with Stalin. But then Hitler invaded Russia and the Second World War became "a People's war". By that time Maurice had already joined the New Zealand Division where he and my father became comrades in arms. Later again – I think in 1956 when the Russians went into Hungary – he left the Party.

On that hilltop above Titirangi Maurice was pointing out to me where the different suburbs lay and the main thoroughfares, the little matchbox structure lit by orange lights that was the Harbour Bridge in the far distance, patches of shadow that were hills and parks, water and islands; and gradually I became conscious of something different in his voice. It was gentle, almost caressing. I thought, He must love Auckland. And then it began to creep over me that, yes, he did, but he was using that feeling in some way to impress me, or to affect me. It was a surprise. It made me think of something I'd noticed about Maurice and Lee Lomas, a way they had of joking together, mocking one another, and touching as they passed in a crowded room, that was intimate, conspiratorial. Until that moment I hadn't thought anything of this because it didn't seem to be hidden from Dick or to bother him.

Maurice had fallen silent now, standing beside me looking

out towards the huge darkness of the Manukau Harbour.

I said it was time we went back to the house.

In response he quoted,

> Always, in these islands, meeting and parting
> Shake us, making tremulous the salt-rimmed air

and then he laughed, as if to say "Don't take me seriously – this is just a game."

He went ahead of me, knowing the track off the summit better than I did. But for just a moment before we reached the paved road he stopped and half turned so I was checked on the narrowest part of the path, with manuka pressing in above on either side. It was like Dan, the first night we met, stopping in front of me on the path up from the tennis court and turning towards me as the lights went out. But the feeling was different. Dan had seemed tentative – or anyway not threatening; whereas now, out of the darkness came this strong impression of confidence and challenge. I wasn't frightened of Maurice – I was excited; but at the same time my brain, or my instincts, moved very quickly. I didn't stop, and I didn't go faster. Somehow in the dark I found my way round him, sliding on the smooth damp clay that sloped up from the track, but getting by without touching him, as if I'd noticed nothing.

Down from the hill and back at the house I played table tennis with him. Dan was helping Lee prepare a meal. They were frying what Lee called hamburger steaks while Richard and Rosie made a salad in a big wooden bowl. Dick was outside collecting pine cones for a fire. The steaks were put into bread rolls and we ate them with the salad, sitting around a big scrubbed table and drinking beer which Dan had brought in from his car. It wasn't really cold, but Dick lit his fire, first with manuka, then heaping up the pine cones. After coffee we did the dishes together, bumping into one another in the small kitchen.

76

Maurice suggested another game of table tennis. We played one game, and then another and another. Sometimes he won, sometimes I did. I knew we should stop – it wasn't sociable to go on and on like this – but each time Maurice said "One more game?" I agreed. It was something to do with that excitement I'd felt up on the hilltop.

Dan came in, restless, and roamed about the room, not saying anything.

"One more game, Comrade," Maurice said, and again I agreed. Dan walked out. I heard his car starting up and saw its headlights among the trees on the drive as he rolled down to the road.

"Little tantrum?" Maurice said – and served the ball.

Half an hour later Dan was back and I was waiting for him on the verandah.

He was silent at the wheel. After only a short distance he turned off the main road on to one that curved down towards the bays on the Manukau Harbour. He parked under pines and got out. I followed him into the plantation. The air was cool but not cold, fresh and still and full of pine fragrance. As we walked a half moon appeared and disappeared in the gaps between the trees. After a time we sat down in a thick bed of pine needles and had our first real quarrel. It was about nothing – unimportant things, long since forgotten, but disputed angrily. Maurice Scobie was mentioned, but only in passing. Then we made love, but with a kind of violence, as if the quarrel was continuing.

*　　*　　*

Every Thursday lunchtime in one of the university lecture theatres there was a student forum which had gradually been taken over by the protest movement. Terry Scobie and Ros came with their Alsatian dog, Ho. Terry was a good speaker with a broad grin and a strong line in heavy irony. Ros was more violent. She shouted and cajoled, which made Ho, sensing her anger and confused by it, bark at the audience, baring his teeth in a snarl that parodied Ros's manner. Sometimes Justin Pope came with them and read his poems. He was also to be seen sitting barefoot and cross-legged in the quadrangle, or under a tree in the park, chanting his mantras or silent in contemplation, a peace sign or a few flowers laid out on the ground in front of him.

Laura thought Steve Casey the best of the student speakers. He was more academic than Terry, made fewer jokes, didn't go out of his way to charm his audience; but he always impressed her – he was so tough-minded and relentless.

That was the year of the biggest of the marches against the war. The student group set off from Princes Street, the trade unionists and others from the bottom of Queen Street, and the two columns converged on the Town Hall. No one could remember a protest march in Auckland that had drawn so many thousands of people. Laura walked between Dan and Steve. At first it was solemn, almost funereal. Then from far off, as they moved down towards Queen Street, came the chants and shouts of the other column. The noise got louder, the two seeming to call and answer one another. She felt a nervous excitement in herself and all around her. As the two groups flowed together, filling the street, there was a feeling of exhilaration and of power, as if this time something might be achieved, someone in office might listen, and the country draw back from its involvement in the war.

There had been a shower of rain, and when the crowd gathered outside the town hall Laura looked up and saw lights shivering in rain drops hanging from the leaves of a tree in a big tub. As the crowd swayed this way and that, and the tree swayed with it, the drops shone and shivered and fell. There was a good clean madness in the air, an intoxication that seemed, for as long as it lasted, to justify itself almost without need of Vietnam or any other cause.

78

Afterwards Laura and Dan drove with others out to Titirangi, to the house of Jake and Ruth Izen, friends of the Lomases, where they all sat drinking and talking about the war and the protest and "what might happen". Maurice Scobie was there, and Dick and Lee and their children.

The Lomases and the Izens were saying that America couldn't win; but on the other hand no President would accept defeat. All they could see for Vietnam, stretching away into the future, was more conflict, worse destruction.

But Maurice didn't agree. "You have to face it – America will win; Ho Chi Minh will be defeated. What Spain was to the 'thirties, Vietnam will be to the 'sixties and 'seventies. And maybe winning or losing isn't so important as we all think."

There was a ripple of indignation. "What is important?" Lee wanted to know.

"I'm not sure," Maurice said. "In the Party we used to call it the Struggle."

"You sound like my father," Laura said.

"Like Vince?" Maurice protested. "How is that possible?"

"He believes in the One Great Scorer who marks not that you won or lost but how you played the game."

Maurice laughed, but he stuck to his guns. The problem was that when you were on the winning side, you were also responsible for what followed. "That's why the truly great causes are the lost ones."

The others were indignant – they weren't listening to him any more. But as he said it, Laura remembered those perfect crystal drops swaying among the leaves over the heads of the crowd.

She looked straight at him. "Maybe you're right," she said. "It's the energy that matters, not the outcome."

★　　★　　★

Jake and Ruth Izen had built their house in bush at the top of a hill not far from the Scenic Drive. The lower rooms looked out into a dim, beautiful brown-green world of trunks, tree ferns and leaf mould that had a submarine feel about it. The upper rooms and the decks that opened off them offered long views through and over the treetops, as from the hill Laura had climbed with Maurice. The Izens went in for beautiful interiors, polished floors, Danish furniture, hand-woven rugs, pottery, modern paintings, fine dishes and exotic cooking. But they also had a bach on the West Coast in a grassy hollow shaded by pohutukawas and close to the sea, and the group gathered there at weekends, swimming in summer, taking long bush walks in winter, sleeping overnight in bunks and on camp stretchers.

It was a still, clear, cloudless and moonless night late in April. Laura was sitting out on a deckchair looking up at the night sky when she became aware that someone had come out to join her.

"This seat taken?" he asked, and she recognized Maurice's voice.

"Give it a try," she suggested.

The canvas stretched and the chair creaked as he sat down.

"Vacant," he reported; and for a long time – so long it produced in her a curious drowsiness, as if simply Maurice's presence, or the knowledge of it, was faintly hypnotic – they sat silent. The stars prickled and throbbed, the planets shone. The Southern Cross, in that clear air, seemed to hang forward out of the sky at a rakish angle. A morepork repeated itself in a nearby tree and got an answer from the hills behind.

"It's when you look up there," Maurice said, "you know it's important to insist that there's no God. Otherwise it's just banal. Everything is banality. The big magician made it all – for himself, and for us. He stuck us on this piece of revolving rock to look at it and admire it and praise him for his power and his benevolence . . ."

Laura could think of nothing to say to this, and after a moment he went on.

"Beauty's the problem. We used to say in the Party that beauty was a factor of utility. But what's useful about the stars? As a system of street lighting they're inadequate. As aids to navigation they're obsolete. So why are they beautiful? But look. There they are."

And there they were. She stared up into the glittering silence and felt faint. They'd tramped a long way that day, but that didn't explain her feeling of weakness. It was as if tiredness had left her open to the influence of the sky, and of Maurice's voice – unprotected against them.

"I try to imagine it all without the human race here to look at it," he said, "and that's difficult. Imagine the whole universe just as it is, all those lovely lights without anyone or anything able to see and to know."

The voice came to her as if she wasn't there; or as if it didn't matter who was there.

"A spoonful of God and you spoil the flavour. You destroy the mystery. 'When I was a child I spake as a child, I understood as a child, I thought as a child, but when I became a man I put away childish things.' The first childish thing you put away is big daddy who made heaven and earth."

And again, a little later: "It's a cooling star, the sun. We know that now. It must be a new point in the history of the human mind. First we had to come to terms with the fact that we could wipe ourselves out. Now we learn that time will do it anyway. There will have been this single speck of consciousness in the vastness of space, and then nothing. Can you imagine that? It seems to me so exciting, and so mysterious. We have the best seats in the house. We can look at it all up there and feel the wonder of it. But the price of admission is death." He laughed. "We should be kind to one another. Planet Earth is the universal lifeboat, and it's leaking."

Now the silence lasted so long she thought he must have gone to sleep. But perhaps she was the one who slept, because after a time she realized the chair beside her was empty. She went indoors. In the bach they were lounging about, exhausted from the day's walk, talking, drinking beer. Maurice wasn't there, and nor was Lee.

Next morning she was woken by gun shots. She detached herself from Dan who was still sleeping, and pushed aside the ragged curtain over the window beside her bunk. Up the grassy slope that sheltered the hollow from winds off the sea was an old wooden sign that read "Happy Valley". It shuddered as each shot went through it. At the outer edges bits of wood flew off. She craned her head to see where the shots were coming from. Dick Lomas was sitting in the grass with a .22 rifle, loading and firing at the sign. His face was neither grim nor smiling – just businesslike.

★    ★    ★

Laura writes:

Our walk had taken us down through a valley to a part of the coast inaccessible by road. We parked our cars some miles down an unsealed road and went into a well-beaten track through manuka. The grey-brown stems with flaky bark had no foliage for ten or twelve feet, then opened out overhead to make a canopy. It was a bright day, and sunlight, where it found gaps, came through in dramatic shafts and splashes. There was something military about those hundreds of thousands of manuka stems – not regimented, because their lines and angles were irregular, but I remember "legion" was the word that came into my mind as I looked at them.

We went in single file down the track – Jake and Ruth, then Dick and Lee ahead and behind Richard and Rosie,

Maurice next, and finally Dan and I – at first throwing remarks back and forth along the line, but after a time falling into the silent rhythm of a long walk.

We came to a fork in the track and a sign saying "Pararaha Valley: For Experienced Trampers Only". Here we cut ourselves manuka stakes to help stay upright on the steeper slopes. Soon the manuka ended and we were in the bush, mostly kauri, but alternating with groves of nikau palms and puriri, bearded with epiphytes and hung with vines. At our first stop in one of these groves Richard and Rosie picked up nikau fronds and used them as sledges, riding them down the steep slopes.

At the top of the valley that ran down towards the coast the track turned to follow the river and became less clearly marked. There were any number of what looked like paths on either side, but it was often impossible to be sure which was the one we should follow. Again and again when the river dropped dangerously among boulders and over falls, with sheer rock rising on either side, we would leave it and follow a track that seemed to take us over and around the bluff, only to find that it petered out in dense undergrowth or came to a steep drop and stopped. Climbing up and then back on these false trails exhausted us, and we decided it was best to stay with the river.

Sometimes we were forced to wade because there was no foothold on either side; and sometimes to climb down falls over rock worn smooth and covered with a fine slippery mould. Once, when Jake had lost his foothold and been carried a short way down rapids, we talked about turning back; but now it seemed less effort, and no more dangerous, to go with gravity than to climb back up into the hills. And although we had become wary and uncertain, there were moments of exhilaration when a turn in the valley opened up a new view, more dramatic and beautiful than the last. We were catching glimpses of the ocean now, and of dunes stretching away in a haze of spray and sunlight down the four or five miles to the sand bar at the entrance to the Manukau Harbour.

It was well into the afternoon when we reached the valley floor. We were still in bush, but the track was well marked. At a clearing by a pool we stopped and ate sandwiches and chocolate and apples. Dick and the children swam. Maurice and Lee strolled down the track and out of sight. I took photographs, which I still have.

Soon after that the bush gave way to low scrub, grass, flax and toi-toi. The river ambled, broadening, turning this way and that across flat land. The sea was out of sight, hidden by dunes that reared up like beautifully sculpted hills; and the boom of the surf beyond seemed to come from behind as it echoed off the rocky bluffs on either side of the valley. The river, caught now on the flats between dunes and cliffs, spread out and became a vast shallow swamp, clear and still, bristling with green water grasses and raucous with frogs.

Gradually the sandhills levelled off, held stable by marram grass. Richard and Rosie scrambled up the shifting difficult slope, we followed, and there at last was the ocean, blue and white and green, rolling shoreward in long lines and breaking on a beach that glinted black and white.

It was there that Dan and I were separated for a time from the others – I think we just waved them on ahead, and shouted that we would follow. He lay under a pohutukawa, while I explored a tunnel that was part of an old logging track. I came back and, I suppose, kissed him, or ruffled his hair, and told him I loved him.

And that's where he chose to end his writing, leaving us there, Dan Cooper and Laura Jackson under pohutukawas, frozen in time like the lovers on the Grecian urn. Why? Not, I think, because he couldn't have gone on, but because, let's say, beyond that point lay only a severance which would seem to require explanation, and for which none, or none which mightn't seem to involve apportioning blame, could be offered.

"Everything comes out white." Dan was right to stop where he did. It was the limit of his understanding, because, thus far at least, and perhaps for ever, it is the limit of my imagining.

   ★  ★  ★

I dream that Maurice has taken me to a farm. I'm in a field with horses. A Maori comes along, introduces himself, leans forward. I realize he wants me to hongi, feel reluctant, but I do it. The nose is warm and soft and a good feeling passes between us. Then I hongi with another, younger Maori. We go indoors. There's an older man who looks Pakeha but I see that he is also of Maori descent and he too moves to hongi. His nose is jet black and shiny like a dog's. There must be something wrong with it and I feel revulsion, but I know I must touch noses, and when I do, once again there's good feeling – everything is all right. A woman is standing at a wood range cooking, a Pakeha who watches but takes no part. I see no Maori women. Maurice has vanished from the dream. I hear a piano being played and know it's Dan. I go looking for him. It's a rambling derelict farmhouse with sash windows and wide verandahs. There are saddles, harness, bridles, gumboots, gum-spears, rifles, heaped in corners. Hens wander on and off the verandahs and even in and out of the rooms. I can see a vegetable garden protected by a manuka-brush fence. Dogs are tied under the macrocarpas. It's all so familiar, I'm not sure why; and all the time there's the beautiful sound of a Beethoven sonata being played on a piano which I can't find. The house rambles on, offering room after room, but no piano, no pianist.

I half wake myself and wonder what it means. I can hear Jacob crooning to himself in his cot in the next room. I dream again, but now, as I see myself wandering through the house, I'm also describing it to Steve Casey, asking him to explain it. Steve begins to lecture. He goes on at great length. I'm impressed – what he has to say seems so right and so perceptive. I force myself to wake, and to bring with me the memory of what Steve has been saying, but I'm left only with meaningless fragments.

In the half-light I see Roger is already out of bed. He pulls the curtains apart and looks out. "You awake? It's going to be a cracker." He turns to look at me. "You've been talking in your sleep."

I ask what I've been saying, and he tells me, "Just mutterings. Something about a flute, I think."

A flute! I tell him about my dream – that I had to hongi.

"That's not a dream," Roger says. "That's a nightmare."

I tell him it had a nice atmosphere. I say nothing of the piano, and my certainty that Dan was playing it.

He goes through to the bathroom. Above the noise of the shower he sings, tunelessly.

Still only half-awake, I think about Dan. An image comes to mind – a memory that's like a dream. Dan and I are naked, sitting on a bed. Beams of sunlight are coming into the room, dust floating in them. Everything is still and quiet. There's no sense of urgency. He's leaning back among cushions, looking down where I'm holding the end of his penis, half erect in my hand, my thumb moving slowly back and forth across the shaft. I too am looking down. It's a moment that seems to have no beginning and no end. The thumb moves back and forth, slowly, on and on into eternity, like those numbers, our respective ages, his and mine, for ever reducing by simple addition to the same single digit.

\*     \*     \*

86

The first year away from home was difficult. Vince was always about, uneasy, worrying whether I was eating properly, studying seriously, practising my tennis. I thought he didn't approve of my association with Dan; but he said little, probably because he blamed himself for starting it.

Winter came and went. Spring brought examinations, and early summer, their results. I had passed all my papers, easily and well if not brilliantly, and I was satisfied with that. Now the warm weather was back I played some tennis, but it no longer seemed serious. When Vince told me I didn't care enough about winning I quoted

> For when the One Great Scorer comes
> To write against your name,
> He marks – not that you won or lost
> But how you played the game

He looked baffled. That, he told me, was a verse for bunnies, not for someone who had it in her to be a champion. Soon he gave me up as a tennis player and turned his attentions to my brother and sister.

Dan and I spent days and often weekends at the west coast. Now it seemed as if all of us knew that Maurice was having an affair with Lee, though still no one said it aloud. It must have been partly because of uncertainty about Dick. He always seemed relaxed, amiable, sleepy, unsuspicious. It was impossible to believe he didn't notice what everyone else noticed. So did he not care? Or did he know what was happening, and its limits, and that it was no cause for concern?

And there was something else that was peculiar. Maurice continued to send me signals which I didn't encourage but, despite myself, I enjoyed. He never seemed to require any particular response. And in her own style Lee played the same game with Dan. She reached out and touched him when they met. She danced with him at parties, close and

87

affectionate. She cuddled up to him when we sat round a fire. She smoothed his hair and warmed her hands under his sweater. But it was always Lee and Maurice who went missing on walks, took a different car together and arrived late when there was somewhere to go, disappeared from a party and came back looking flushed and ruffled. And all the time Dick appeared sanguine, benign, faintly mocking, making jokes that had only the slightest edge of malice. There had been that one occasion at the bach when I had woken to see him shooting holes in the Happy Valley sign – otherwise nothing to suggest that he was suffering.

And then it happened. Dick simply declared – first to Lee and the children, later to the rest of us – that he wanted a divorce. He was in love with a young married woman at the scientific establishment where he worked. The woman's husband had found out about their affair and now Dick was returning to the States just as soon as it could be arranged, taking the woman with him.

Lee talked to her friends, individually and together, and wept. We consoled her as best we could, and wondered about her association with Maurice. When that was hinted at she shrugged it off. It was nothing. She didn't care about Maurice. He seemed baffled by this, and distressed, but she avoided him, would scarcely speak to him. To Dan once, as they walked along the beach apart from the others and enclosed in the noise of surf, she said Maurice was "an old man". "You were the one," she said. Dan pretended not to have heard, and afterwards, when he told me, he wasn't certain whether that was what she had said.

In only a few weeks, it seemed, Dick was on a plane out with his new partner, and Lee and the children moved into the Happy Valley bach while she made her own plans to return. In fact, she remained there for another year, supported by friends, and by cheques sent by Dick's parents who would be glad, Lee believed, that the marriage was over, but concerned about their grandchildren's welfare . . .

★   ★   ★

Long ago I tried to write about that time. It was to be a novel or a novella – "an extended fiction" (to use Steve Casey's phrase). That was after Roger and I were married and I was pregnant. I wanted – was it to put all that experience behind me? Or to make some use of it, not to let it go to waste? I enjoyed the writing, and even thought I was doing it well. And then I had to stop for some reason – I think it was when the baby arrived – and after that, whenever I thought about what I'd written I felt it didn't belong to me, rejected it, couldn't even bring myself to read it. I put it away in a cupboard, and even now, after all these years, that's where it sits.

Well, if I learn nothing else from my study of Hilda Tapler at least I know now that that rejection is something to be overcome, not indulged. She wrote her fiction, she said, not to invent what never happened but as a way of understanding what did. Then she would turn against it, unable to read it or even to look at it. While she was living in England she told a writer-friend about this, thinking she was describing something peculiar to herself. But the reply was only, "Of course" – dismissively. This was just a part of the process, which many writers – possibly most – experienced.

Finding that in Hilda's journal convinced me I should go back and read what I wrote all those years ago. I haven't done it yet, but I will.

But there was an event I didn't even try to include in my fiction, because it frightened me; and even now I find it difficult to recall in detail, not because I've forgotten but because I remember too clearly, and the recollection, when I concentrate on it, upsets me. It was after Dick had gone

89

back to America, and Lee was living in the bach on the west coast with Richard and Rosie . . .

★    ★    ★

It was after Dick had gone back to America and Lee was living in the bach on the west coast with Richard and Rosie. The bach was among the dunes, close to the road. There was a sandy garden. Some pohutukawas, some flax, a few flowering bushes, managed to find soil and sustenance. The wind blew in from the sea, surf pounded on the beach, spray drifted up and over refracting the sun's rays as they slanted across the clifftops to the north.

It was swimming weather, but it was a weekday and the beach was empty. There were no surf patrols, though one or two lifesavers were up at the clubhouse. Laura and Dan were visiting and they got ready to swim with Lee and the children. Richard and Rosie were ready first, and Laura walked with them down a path through dunes to the beach, expecting Dan and Lee to follow at any moment. It was a sunny day, the tide was low and there was a big surf, the waves seeming to hang high and motionless for a moment before dumping themselves on the flattened sand, so the noise was heard instantly, and then a second time, a boom echoing off the cliff faces.

The sand shelved only gradually and though Richard and Rosie were soon well out from the beach they were only up to their thighs except when a wave dumped down on them, rolling them over and back towards the shore. Laura followed, looking back expecting to see Dan and Lee coming through the dunes but there was still no sign of them. And then there was a rush of water, outward. Laura felt it first along the sand, around her ankles, then at her knees as the full volume of water dragged at her. She saw Richard leaning forward, staying upright, facing the shore and trying to walk, not succeeding, but holding his own

90

against the rush. But Rosie, shrieking now, was swept off her feet.

Laura let her legs float up and at once she was swept towards the struggling girl. She got hold of her and tried to bring her feet down to the sand but now it was too late – the force of the water made it impossible, and they were being swept along, as if a giant gap had opened through the lines of surf and they were riding through it on an express train, straight out towards open water.

She clung to Rosie, getting her upright so they floated or sailed together through the turbulent area and out into a broad, beautiful blue-green swell that lifted them high up and, passing, sent them down deep into the trough. "Raise your hand," Laura said. "Right up – high as you can." It was hard to speak without swallowing water; and she couldn't easily hold her own hand up while supporting Rosie with the other. Rosie wasn't panicking but her face was tense and white with fear, and when she tried to hold her hand up her head sank beneath the water.

With each lift that gave them a view of the beach Laura looked for Dan and Lee. She didn't see them. The beach seemed empty except for a scurrying figure she knew was Richard. He had made it ashore and now he was running, bent double as if in pain, making not for the bach but for the clubhouse.

Still the rip was carrying them away from the shore, though more slowly now. Laura thought she should move, not against the flow which she knew would exhaust her, but sideways, out of it. But the effort distressed Rosie, who took one mouthful, then a second, and began to thrash about. The energy required to calm her and hold her up left Laura with none to spare.

The struggle seemed to go on and on, and then all at once time ceased to be something measurable, long or short. Laura's consciousness entered a zone of something like numbness, where the sense of effort and pain and exhaustion and nausea were present but anaesthetized. She could recognize them but no longer feel them; or she felt them but didn't suffer. Her mind drifted. She had no will, except just the knowledge that she should try to stay afloat, head above water, and keep hold of Rosie. And Rosie too, after a last panic flurry, seemed to be drifting inside herself. The look of fear had gone. Her head lolled, as if she were falling asleep. At some moment, Laura thought, I'm going to lose the ability to care what happens, and she'll just drift away from me. My fingers will let her go, and she'll float away and die. And then, after a while, I'll die too.

Now she saw herself from above. She was looking down seeing the top of her own head and Rosie's – two straw-coloured aureoles of hair floating out in a half-circle to the side and behind each face, two bathing suits, one green, one red, two sets of arms, two sets of legs pale, refracted and wavering in the clean, dark, fizzing water – and she thought, looking down, how odd, neither of us is wearing a cap . . .

When she came back to consciousness on the beach, she saw first an orange-capped lifesaver bending over her, and Dan's face beyond the cap. She couldn't speak, and she was sure Rosie must be dead, until she heard Lee's voice somewhere nearby. "Oh, my poor little Rosella-chick. Poor baby. What were you thinking of? Lie there, baby. Keep still. Oh my god, Honey, you gave us such a fright. We thought you were dead."

*　　*　　*

There was an exchange I had with Dan, more than once, which went roughly as follows:

"Where were you?"

"We were coming."

"Why so long?"

"Lee decided she was wearing the wrong bathing suit. It was ripped or something. She had to change."

"Did she need help?"

Silence.

"I'm sure she wanted it."

"What?"

"Help. From you. Getting changed . . ."

"Jesus, Laura, we didn't know you'd let them go in."

"I didn't let them. They're not my kids."

Silence.

"So now it's my fault, is it, that Rosie nearly drowned? I thought I saved her life."

"You did. You were marvellous. You . . ."

"It wasn't just Rosie . . ."

"I know."

"I nearly drowned, Dan."

"Don't even say it. It's too . . ."

"Because Lee was changing her bathing suit."

"Laura, it could have happened anyway . . ."

"You know what Lee is? She's . . ."

"You're upset."

"She's a predator."

Silence.

"Yes, I'm upset. It upsets me to talk about it. I've told you that."

"You saved a life."

"Let's change the subject."

"The surfies said . . ."

"Dan, can we please talk about something else?"

And so on.

It did upset me to talk about it, and mostly I avoided the subject. There was a feeling like cold marble that came with the memory. I had never been so close to death. Rosie's death – that was one kind of horror; but also my own – that was another, darker, more mysterious, more chilling. And the thought that this had happened while Lee changed into another bathing suit, while Dan (or so I imagined) watched and smirked . . .

One night I dreamed that I was with Lee and the children. Dan wasn't there, and in the dream, although I knew someone was missing, I couldn't recall who it was. Lee kept laughing in a way I found sinister and saying she'd changed Rosie's name. Rosie was to be called Rosmersholm. And then she laughed and said, "No, not Rosmersholm. She's going to be called Little Eyolf."

I woke, it was morning and I was in Dan's bed. I wondered why these names from Ibsen's plays had figured in my dream. Rosmersholm was like Rosie – at least it started with Ros. But why Little Eyolf? I thought I might have read the play, or perhaps seen it performed, but I couldn't remember what it was about.

Over breakfast I asked Dan who was Little Eyolf and what happened to him.

"He's a child," Dan said. "A cripple. His parents don't love him, and I think he drowns."

Then he remembered more. "He's crippled because as a baby he was left somewhere precarious by his mother – maybe on a table – while she seduced someone." Dan did a revolving motion with his hand and made a spiralling down noise. "Rolled off the table. Crashed to the floor." Now he must have noticed the expression on my face. "Why?"

I looked hard at him, trying to read him as I told him this. "I dreamed last night that Lee was changing Rosie's name to Little Eyolf."

Dan blinked. That was all.

# FOUR

# 1990 – Three Birthdays

There is an appetite for certainties, but nothing is certain, not even what follows:

Who? My name is Laura Vine Barber.

Where? My address is 26 Rangiview Crescent, Eastern Bays, Auckland.

When? The year is 1990.

1990: In Auckland the Commonwealth Games. At Waitangi, the 150th anniversary of the signing of the Treaty. In the world, the end of the Wall. But in my head, three men I think it's true to say I've loved – Dan, Roger, and (strange even to myself) Maurice – first the anniversaries of their entrances, in three successive months, April, May, June, and then (could it be said?) their exits, by different doors.

★　　★　　★

## 17 April

Dan, half awake in the early morning dark, recovers his dream. He'd been out in a dinghy with Laura, fishing. They came in with their catch – one large eel, which he put down on the sand. Roger came along the beach. Laura had gone, and Roger seemed not to know they'd been out together. The eel was nearly dead and there didn't seem any point in putting it back in the sea – it would die anyway. But as Dan thought this it seemed to shrink a little, as though it knew his thought, and a mark appeared that ran from head to tail, straight down its back which was broad and flat. Dan felt a harsh, cold ache in his foot, and he understood that it was the same pain that was running through the eel's body. Then the creature began to move towards the sea. Roger put his foot in its path, but Dan shouted, "Let it go." The eel moved on; but then again Roger blocked its path, and it lifted its head – not really an eel's head, more a serpent's, with a long jaw, open now, and rows of sharp triangular teeth. It half-snarled, half-spoke, and it wasn't sinister – it was pitiful. It wanted to live. "Let it go," Dan repeated, and the eel slithered forward and reached the water. A small wave washed over it and this time it was away, curving and swimming, half-snake, half-eel, to freedom. Dan walked up the beach to the store. Laura was there. They kissed – a long kiss of infinite tenderness. They walked down the sand. Roger was gone. The dinghy was lying on its side. They turned it over and pushed it into the water.

Awake, Dan holds on to the atmosphere, especially of that kiss. Could you experience anything like it in reality? He feels an unreasonable happiness. He can hear the wind busy and discontented, sighing around the house, finding a loose board it can bang, a window to rattle. He breathes deeply and knows he's in Wellington. The wind will be sweeping in gusts over the ragged hillsides and roughing up the surface of the harbour. Before light begins to come into the room his senses have told him the kind of day it will be, a sky grey and white, turbulent but dry, a sea silver and grey, hillsides dull-green and windswept.

He moves, and remembers now that he's not in his own bed. That's Caroline beside him. He rolls himself over the side of her bed and sits for a moment, elbows on bare knees, chin in his hands, then heaves himself up and goes to the bathroom.

When he comes out of the shower he finds Caroline waiting to go in. "Hullo sailor," she says, and gives his penis a tug.

While he dries himself and shaves she comes and goes, getting herself dressed and ready to go out.

"Don't call a car," she tells him. "I'll drive you. I want to make an early start."

In the kitchen he drinks fruit juice and eats a piece of dry toast. There will be breakfast on the plane. Caroline comes in and ties his tie. He remembers the eel, and the kiss.

"I dreamed about Laura," he says.

"Don't tell me," she says.

He kisses her gently, experimentally, and then more passionately. She laughs and pushes him away. "Are you keeping your eye on the clock?"

While she brings out the car, he puts on his jacket, checks his papers, looks around to be sure he's left nothing.

She toots and he goes out to her. "You don't need to do this," he says; but he gets in.

"I want to do it."

The sky is full of cloud, and full of light. She drives fast, a circuitous route, down into the Aro Valley, up into Brooklyn where she has something to deliver, then down again through back roads that bring them to the sea. Now they're ahead of schedule and she drives more slowly. Waves are shooting up, white and irregular, into the narrow rocky bays.

This road brings them to the back of the domestic terminal, and she parks away from the entrance where they won't be noticed. She kisses him. "*A la prochaine fois?*"

"Yes. We'll make it soon, won't we?" He thinks she would like him to say when, but he feels confused, uncertain from one day to the next what the world will want of him, and what he will want of it.

She reaches over to the back seat for his bag. "Got everything you need?" He takes it, getting out. On an impulse he says, "I didn't tell you – it's my birthday."

"Oh Dan!" She jumps out and comes around the car to where he's standing on the pavement. "Why didn't you say? I would have got a presie."

"At 47 . . . Least said soonest mended."

"That's not true – and you don't mean it."

He kisses her. "I'm an unsatisfactory lover," he acknowledges. "We must work on it."

"I'm not complaining," she says.

On the plane he eats breakfast and works through a sheaf of papers, but the dream sits with him, or over him – an atmosphere, a birthday-gift from the gods.

In Auckland the ministerial car takes him through town and over the Harbour Bridge to the North Shore; then off the motorway and along the road that runs through the east coast bays. The Takapuna shopping centre is being repaved in fancy squares and fitted out with new street-lighting – white balls on arrangements of painted metal piping. There are new shops and office buildings. It's part of the boom the Government he belongs to has created, which all the indicators say has come to a stop but in Auckland seems to be running on like a headless chicken.

As he thinks this, and feels it, he knows that it contradicts his own beliefs and actions as a member of the Government. But he doesn't enjoy seeing the wood and corrugated iron, which belonged to his childhood and still seem to him romantic, replaced by these anonymous replicas of international commerce.

They reach the bay where the Barbers live, locate the house, and drive down to the shopping centre. He takes from his bag the envelope containing "The Magic Bagwash", puts on his shades, hoping to pass unnoticed, gives his instructions to the driver, and walks back up the hill.

★      ★      ★

> My birthday began with the water-
> Birds and the birds of the winged trees flying my name
> Above the farms and the . . .

No. His birthday began, it might be said, with an advertisement in the *Herald*. It read "Roger Marley Barber is 40 Today", and there was a photograph of him in a barbecue apron, winking and giving the thumbs up. Across the apron was printed "Corporation Lawyer – Charge Your Glasses".

Who was responsible? Not I, said Laura – and he must have known it wasn't her style. They might have suspected her father, except that since his stroke the ginger had gone out of Vince. More likely it was Roger's mates in the firm. Anyway he was pleased, he liked it – didn't she?

Laura laughed and pulled a face. Angela and Ben were impressed – Daddy was in the paper. They cut it out and stuck it to the fridge door. Jacob pointed and said "Door" because that was his newest word.

The phone rang while they were at breakfast. Roger went to it, smiling. The half of the conversation Laura could hear went:

"Thanks, Dad. Yes, so they say. Life begins at, and all that . . . Yes, I know you did . . . It was good, wasn't it? . . . Yes . . . Oh, you saw it . . . No, I don't know who . . . Well, come on now. I'm not on the bench . . . Yes, of course, but times have . . . You have to accept . . . I didn't think . . . Don't be such a . . . This is my birthday . . ."

Laura raised her eyebrows at him across the room. Roger's smile was gone. His father was one of an old legal school who believed in the sacredness of wigs and gowns and didn't approve of fast money. *Après Dad, le déluge!*

"OK. Yes." Roger sounded weary now. "All well, thanks . . . I will. I'll tell her that . . . Thanks for your call.

Yes, you too. And love to Mother when she gets back."

Laura said she supposed they ought to try to understand. Gentlemen preferred blondes, and fathers wanted clones.

Roger wasn't sure about that. "If I'd been his kind of academic jurist . . ."

"You think he might have been jealous?"

He sat down and resumed his breakfast. "He's hard to please."

"You know what they thought of him at the Anarchist."

"Because of his ruling on Disorderly Behaviour. Ah, but you see I respect him for that. It's still cited. And they were a whingeing crew."

"Were they? Or were you jealous?"

"Jealous? Well, I was in love with you . . ."

"Past tense?"

"The present goes without saying."

She told him nothing went without saying – least of all love.

He looked at her solemnly. "You're a difficult woman, Laura."

"I'm not your mother, if that's what you mean."

"Oh, come on now, leave her out of it." And of course Laura knew he was right.

He lifted Jacob out of his high chair and set him free to follow Ben out of doors. "I didn't tell you," he said (changing the subject, she supposed – or was it a small revenge?) "the joke Ginny told me the other night. Question: what are the two words Maori has contributed to the English language? Answer: mana, and paranoia."

Laura frowned and began to clear away the children's plates. "Ginny should know better," she said; but she wasn't sure whether it was the joke she was objecting to, or its source.

\*　　　\*　　　\*

100

The old man walked off Queen Street into the building that was called Mid City. He caught sight of himself in a mirror and tried to think of himself as old. He didn't succeed, and arithmetic didn't help. He'd had his three score years and ten – plus two. So what? He still looked spry and felt healthy. He reminded himself that he might be dying, and that didn't help either. If it was true (and he veered about, sometimes feeling doomed, at others that he would "fight this thing" and live for ever) he could only see himself as viable, but invaded. Something foreign had taken up residence in his body. Either it would win or he would, and according to his doctors, who might or might not be telling the truth, the chances were about even. That meant (simple arithmetic again) worse, much worse, than the chances at Russian roulette. How would you like your life to depend on the toss of a coin? No, it was better to accept that death was on its way, like a parcel posted somewhere abroad, probably to come by sea, possibly but less likely by air, with a faint but negligible chance that it might be lost or destroyed or go to the wrong address. Then every day it didn't arrive could be treated as a bonus; and when it did you would be ready.

Shakespeare had some lines about that, and the old man (Maurice called himself an old man again, for the good, he told himself, of his mortal soul) had looked them up:

Be absolute for death: either death or life
Shall thereby be the sweeter. Reason thus with life:
If I do lose thee, I do lose a thing
That none but fools would keep.

That was that pompous Duke in *Measure for Measure*, but it was comforting enough in its wordy way. It had consoled the young Claudio, about to be executed. But Maurice had read on, remembering that the consolation didn't last; and soon Claudio was pleading with his sister to give herself to Lord Angelo, who had condemned him, and thus save his life:

> Ay, but to die, and go we know not where;
> To lie in cold obstruction, and to rot;
> This sensible warm motion to become
> A kneaded clod . . .

There was something invigorating in the harshness of that. Going up the escalator Maurice said it over again. "To lie in cold obstruction and to rot." He was smiling as he reached the top, which he thought of (wondering at his own excess of literariness) as *"al som de l'escalina"*.

Last night he'd dreamed that he was walking with Ulla under copious trees in an enclosed garden in London, where they first met. He'd looked down and seen a scorpion on his trouser leg. He tried to brush it away but it clung with its horrible stick legs and hooks, and reared up at him, ready to strike. He'd woken in the dark, alone, afraid. Unable to sleep, he'd walked about, made tea, felt sorry for himself, wished his marriage to Ulla had lasted. It was his fault it had not. His affair with Lee Lomas had been the last straw. Twenty years ago. Twenty years of sexual adventuring. It was no use whimpering now and wanting to be mothered. He'd resolved to regret nothing . . .

Ginny was waiting for him at one of the tables that looked over Queen Street. She hugged him and wished him a happy birthday. From this one floor up they liked to sit watching people down in the street.

Maurice had told her next to nothing about his recent medical adventures and the threat that now hung over him. As long as he looked and felt normal he didn't want her treating him in some special way.

"Why don't they eat cake?" he said, as they carried their

trays to the table. "It was a good question, wasn't it? And now look – they do."

"We do," she corrected.

He acknowledged the correction. "We do."

She looked at what they'd selected. "Hopeless," she said. "I want to stay thin, but I have this serious cake deficiency."

Maurice quoted, "It was as if God said, 'Let there be cake', and there was cake, and God saw that it was good."

"Mansfield?"

"Mansfield."

"'At the Bay'?"

He shook his head. "I can't remember which story, but not 'At the Bay'."

He looked at her across the table, smiled, and took her hand. "Good heavens, Ginny, you're a beautiful young woman."

*　　*　　*

May 12th was a Saturday, and for his party Roger's friends in the firm, now its senior partners, had taken over the Martello Towers Entertainment Suite on the floors above their own.

Laura tried hard to enjoy it, then to pretend she had. She didn't like to seem the puritan. People had to be able to unwind, to entertain themselves in their own way. Going over it afterwards she tried to weigh it up, to stick to facts. First, there was the invitation. It said, "Men black tie, women black stockings." What did it mean?

It was a joke, for Christ's sake (that was Roger); and yes, she could see that it was. But even jokes had to mean something, didn't they?

Was she humourless, as he said? No, she knew that wasn't true. But it was true their humours didn't match.

The security guard on Queen Street let the guests through

as they flashed their invitations, and they were ferried in groups up to the 24th floor, where they emerged into half light, full volume, a bar offering only but endless champagne, and a big sign that read HAPPY BIRTHDAY MARLEY BARBER FROM THE FORTY THIEVES.

The party was on two levels. In the suite's central area a band was playing and there was a dance floor. A curving staircase led up to a mezzanine that looked inward on to the band and the dancers. The air between was filled with coloured balloons, gas-filled and tugging streamers up.

The women (lawyers, secretaries, wives and partners of lawyers) ran, Laura thought, to a pattern – mostly tall, slim, sleek. They'd all spent time and money, as she had, on clothes, hair, makeup, which at intervals they checked and corrected in a hall of mirrors presided over by a young person dressed as something like a Dutch milkmaid.

It was as if the Women's Movement had never happened. That was Laura's first thought. Her second was that these (and again she included herself) were that Movement's products – as surely as this building and what went on in it was the product of Labour's radicalism. When something was "liberated" it seemed that other things shook out into new patterns that had never been part of the plan. It wasn't as if she would have preferred the imaginable alternatives (unshaven legs and armpits? obesity? moralism? dowdiness?). It was just the recognition that another Grand Plan had got wrecked in the execution; and (more to the point) that for her, nothing had changed. She felt, as much as ever, a fish out of water, a square peg in a round hole . . .

But it was nice up there. She enjoyed looking down at the toy cars and the toy ships in port.

She talked first to a lawyer whose black tie was inset with coloured lights that flashed on and off in sequence, powered, as he showed her, from a battery beneath his shirt. He was, he said, almost a neighbour – he lived in the next bay – and

Roger had engaged him on what was now officially called the Tapler Cottage Preservation Project.

Then there was a young doctor called Graham, drinking the champagne as if he thought it mightn't last, who told her how the closed ventilation systems in these buildings produced nose and throat infections, skin conditions, and urinary tract problems which, as long as the sufferer went on working in the building, could only be treated, not cured.

"I try to think of it as my professional spin-off from the corporate life-style, but really it's just a fashionable insanity. Why in Auckland, with no extremes of heat or cold, have windows that can't be opened?"

And then they talked about books.

When it came time for what were called "the formalities" everyone was more or less drunk. The firm's senior partner made the speech. Roger was "the biggest prick in the profession". He was also "the nicest guy in the game". He knew how to "pick a winner" (this, Laura could see she was to understand, was a reference to her). He had "a heart of silver" which, however, he sometimes "wore on his sleeve".

It was interspersed with cheers and shouts, and an occasional drum roll. The climax brought in a huge pink cardboard cake on wheels, with forty blue cardboard candles topped with red cellophane flames, and round its sides the mottoes ROGERING ON and HERE'S TO THE ROARING FORTIES. The crowd sang Happy Birthday, and at the end of it, following another drum roll, a girl in fishnet tights and a top hat sprang out of the cake and embraced Roger so vigorously she knocked him off the platform.

"What can I say?" he asked, climbing back and taking the microphone. And then what he could say he said at length, thanking Laura (a big cheer) for being at his side, "and also for her backhand"; thanking his "partners in crime", and everyone else, on down what he called "the chain of command", which elicited a shout about being "flushed with success", followed by general cheering and a tuneless "Why was he born so beautiful why was he born at all?"

Laura went through to the bar, not so much for a drink as to get away from the scrimmage and to recover. She found the young doctor holding himself up, his back to the bar, his elbows on its marble top. "Nice party," he said, frowning.

For what seemed a long peaceful few minutes they stood looking at the lights and darkness beyond the windows. Because he was drunk and she not perfectly sober, there was no need for talk. When Graham spoke he seemed to be picking out his words one by one.

"Have you noticed – *Laura* . . ." He turned to check he'd got the name right. "In American movies – have you noticed people don't just ask a question? They say 'Do you mind if I ask a question?' Doesn't it strike you as odd? I mean, 'Do you mind if I ask a question?' is a question. So what if the other person says no?"

"You mean says yes."

He looked puzzled. She said, "You mean what if the other person says 'Yes, I do mind'."

He sighed and closed his eyes for a while. Then he asked whether she read a lot of novels.

"Quite a lot. What about you?"

"Same. A lot. I keep one in the top drawer of my desk at the surgery. Do you know Freud's theory about fiction? He said people wrote it to deal with loss."

She told him Hilda Tapler had said she wrote fiction because it was the only thing in her life she could control.

"Good." He nodded. "Still I think I prefer Freud's . . ." His voice faded, and then he said quite audibly, "Anyway, you can't control it."

Laura imagined that top drawer of his surgery desk, half

open. It wasn't a book in there. It was a manuscript. She said, "You write fiction yourself." She was thinking of Chekhov.

He stared at her.

"Don't be alarmed," she said. "I write it too."

★    ★    ★

When Maurice squeezed Ginny's hand and told her she was beautiful he drew on a well of feeling that was deeper than she knew or could understand, because it went back to a time she didn't remember. It was when Terry and Ros were living with their friends in Parnell. Ros became pregnant, not for the first time, but now she decided she wanted to have a baby. It was safely born; but their lives in that house were so erratic Maurice worried about its welfare. He was told not to fuss, and thought it was probably true that as an old-style Marxist he put too much faith in a disciplined life. After the break-up of his marriage he even tried to adapt to the new order. He grew a wispy Ho Chi Minh beard, shed his tweed jacket and woven tie, and wore a pewter medallion on a chain given to him by Lee Lomas. In cold weather he gave up his old duffle coat and replaced it with a poncho.

And then one day he met Ulla in the street. She tried to talk to him, but she couldn't. Laughter kept bubbling up. She put her hand over her mouth and backed against a fence. "Oh, Maurice," she said. "You look such a clown." After that he went back to his old style, though not to the duffle coat, which was beyond repair and couldn't be replaced.

With Terry and Ros "Peace, brother" was the usual response to any hint of anxiety about the baby. Maurice grew to hate the phrase, and the smell of marijuana, and the apple boxes and demolition doors that served as chairs and tables; and worst of all the endless angry talk about "the

System". He had always thought one of the worst things that could happen to him as a family man was that he might produce children who would do their masters' bidding and grow up to vote National. Now he almost wished it had happened.

He could do nothing about the mess, the irregular hours and meals. What he could do was to offer to mind the baby – christened Ngahuia Rose but somehow, for reasons afterwards forgotten, always called Ginny. So two or three afternoons a week he found himself changing nappies, giving bottles, and "putting her down". He thought at first he was doing it reluctantly, for the child's good and to help the parents; but when he missed an afternoon with her, he felt deprived.

Ginny was healthy and high-spirited. She flourished. Ros and Terry's friends were kind to her. Justin Pope hung Tibetan bells in her cot, chanted mantras and poems over her, and blessed her simultaneously and often in the name of the Lord and the Lord Buddha. Kiev cuddled her and made bright clothes for her.

Maurice walked Ginny in her pushchair. He read her stories, showed her off around the neighbourhood, played with her in the Domain, helped her feed the ducks, bought her toys and showed her dogs and fountains. When she laughed seeing him arrive, or ran up and hugged him around the knees, the heart Ulla told him he lacked turned over.

Then, inevitably, the household broke up. Janet and John left. Justin and Kiev moved north to start a commune on Ninety Mile Beach. Terry was restless. He wanted, as he put it, "to take the agitation nearer to the action" – by which he meant Wellington. He and Ros had friends there, and prospects of congenial work. And so, in what seemed to Maurice only a few days, Ros and Terry had packed their car with everything they owned and set off with little Ginny and the dog, Ho, down the island for the capital.

From time to time he visited Wellington. Ginny was always well and happy; but the bond, so close in his mind, was something the child didn't remember. She liked him in the present, because he was nice to her, and funny – that was all. She had a brother now, and Terry and Ros were married. Terry had found work in radio, and more recently in television. Ros worked part-time for a newspaper. The house had grown more orderly. They had a modern car.

Later again – much later, when Ginny was in her teens – had come the separation. Now Terry was remarried, to one of his fellow producers. Ros worked for a Women's Collective, describing herself as "a political lesbian". She hated Maurice because she hated Terry, and he was Terry's father; or possibly she hated them both because they were male.

Ginny had rebelled against all this, and against her father as well. She had left Wellington and come to Auckland. She was studying law, living on the North Shore in a student flat where they all, she told Maurice staunchly, were resolved to have worldly success and make a lot of money. He took this with several grains of salt. It was her red flag – the banner she sailed under. But he also knew that such flags and banners established patterns that often lasted into middle age, and sometimes a lifetime.

Maurice let her hand go. "Look," he said, pointing down. "In the felt hat."

"An old Leftie," Ginny said. "What a brim!"

For a moment Maurice couldn't speak. Must be weakness, he thought.

"Did you know him?" Ginny asked.

"He was on the Waterfront Executive in '51. A Moscow man. Later a Peking man. Finally probably an Albania man, when there was nowhere else to go."

"Now he looks like Piltdown Man," Ginny said.

Maurice smiled, but he shook his head. "That's too tough, Ginny. He's a good old bugger."

"Salt of the earth," she said, mocking him.

"Salt of the earth," he confirmed.

"I like the hat."

"I used to wear one of those. Before you were born. In the sixties I changed to a sort of sporty tweed thing with a floppy brim. I quite fancied myself in that."

She picked up the peaked cap in soft brown leather he had put down on the chair between them. "I like you in this. It makes you look German."

"Oh my god! I never thought I'd live to hear that as a compliment."

They went back to staring down at the street.

"There's one for you," she said. "In the green – see?" It was a game she played, picking out a new mate for her grandfather. The ones she chose were always young, pretty, expensively dressed, tottering on their heels.

"Too flossy," Maurice said. "I want an intellectual."

"No, you don't. Take her. It's your birthday."

"Well . . . I don't know where I'd keep her . . . All right. She'll do."

But it was too late. The young woman had disappeared into a shop. According to the rules of this nonsense he had to make up his mind before the chosen one went out of sight.

"Too slow," she said.

"You know, don't you – that's a very bad naughty sexist game."

But of course she knew. It was why she played it.

"You've broken a family tradition," Maurice had told her once. "The first conservative in living memory."

But Ginny denied this. "The tradition's revolt," she said. "Your revolt" (she meant his and her parents') "was ideological. I'm in revolt against the ideologies."

And in this, he acknowledged, she was up with the times.

"D'you know," Maurice told her, "my whole life's been governed by a mistake." It was something he couldn't imagine saying to anyone but his granddaughter.

She patted his arm. "Is that painful?"

He thought about it. "Yes and no. You see, there are two Maurice Scobies – the ideologue, and the anarchist. One's upset. The other wants to roll about on the ground and laugh."

"I think it's good." she said. "It's a release – isn't it?"

"Well, yes. I feel I'm released from everything these days. But it's a lesson. It seems in some mysterious way the world is self-correcting. There's no need to interfere – and it doesn't help to try. But we do interfere, of course." And he quoted,

> man, proud man,
> Dress'd in a little brief authority,
> Most ignorant of what he's most assur'd –
> His glassy essence – like an angry ape
> Plays such fantastic tricks before high heaven
> As make the angels weep . . .

"I've been thinking," he went on, "if there was time to write my autobiography I could call it *A Life Well Wasted*. You like that?"

"What do you mean, if there was time?"

He noticed an edge of anxiety in her voice, and was glad of it. For a moment he thought he might tell her. But how much? He thought of the stream of scarlet urine that had signalled the onset of his troubles – the probings, the uncertainty, the X-rays, anaesthetics, discomfort. And the fear. To tell all was always a temptation, and most often a mistake.

"There might be a lot to write," he said. "That's all."

"Oh, if that's all," she said, "you should get on with it."

⋆    ⋆    ⋆

End of party dialogue:

"Can you make this key work, Laura? Nothing works on this . . ."

"You put it in like that. And you turn it. See?"

"Thanks, Chook."

"Why are you getting in on that side?"

"You drive, darling."

"This is new."

"Random checks. I don't think I should take the risk."

"Well, should I?"

"On, driver. *Mush!* Take me home."

"What about a taxi?"

"No taxis."

"Do up your seat-belt, then."

"Fasten seat-belts. Done. Jesus, listen to it."

"What's wrong with it? It's just a big engine."

"I need that BMW."

"You don't."

"To go with . . ."

"With your fortieth birthday?"

"With the fact that I'm – you know . . ."

"The biggest prick in the profession?"

"And the nicest guy in the game. Don't forget that."

"I'll try to forget it, but I know I won't succeed."

"You don't like my mates, do you?"

"Lets' go. It's late."

"No, wait. I know I'm pissed . . ."

"I'm not exactly sober. Let's just . . ."

"Was it so terrible?"

"It was OK, Rodge."

"They work hard . . ."

112

"Yes, yes. And play hard. I know."

"I see."

"'I see.' What does that mean?"

"I've committed another cliché, have I?"

"Please. I'm sorry. I'm a wet blanket."

"These people like me. They trust me."

"And I . . ."

"Laura, don't do that."

"What?"

"Crying. It's not fair."

*　　*　　*

Maurice sat on a bench down at the waterfront, watching the ferries come and go, and a white cruise ship docking at the wharf. It was cool there, but a calm day. On his knee was the book Ginny had given him for his birthday. An old man went slowly up and down, pushing an aluminium walking-frame. One foot dragged. He paused to rest. Maurice looked at him, and the face was familiar. In fact . . .

"Vince!" He could hardly believe it was the same man; and yet there wasn't any doubt. Inside the lines and contours of the old face he could see the young one he'd known in North Africa and again during the Italian campaign.

Vince Jackson stopped, propped on his frame. "Maurice Scobie," Maurice said.

Vince nodded and took his hand. "Had a stroke," he said. "Still don't – ah . . . You know."

"But you remember . . ."

"Oh, I remember you, Scobie. Good fellow. Rebellious bugger. Great times." He nodded and smiled, panting in small pink-cheeked breaths, like a puppy.

"Great times," Maurice agreed. "One shouldn't say it, Vince, but I'm not sorry we had our war."

"The last old . . ." Vince struggled. "You know."

"Soldiers?"

"Soldiers. Real ones."

They smiled at one another, each seeing a strong brown young man in uniform against a tawny landscape.

"Getting over it, are you?" Maurice asked. He meant the stroke, but Vince was trying to add something. He had difficulty remembering some very ordinary words.

"Bit of mystery, isn't it? You and me – like this. I mean in the – you know . . ."

"The war," Maurice ventured.

"The war thing. Fit and active. Still . . ."

Maurice smiled as if he understood. "We're getting on," he said.

"The buggers we left behind. They'd say we were the lucky ones. I mean we – you know . . ."

"Survived."

"Survived." He laughed. Because of his uneven face it was hard to know whether the feeling the laugh released was resigned or bitter. "No more tennis. Now it's time for the one great . . . You know."

But Maurice didn't know what this meant, and was unable to complete the sentence for him.

Vince nodded towards the edge of the paved area. "Girl's waiting. She gives me a trot down here now and . . . Nice to see you, Maurice."

"Good to see you, Vince. Keep at it."

"You too, boy."

Vince pushed his frame on towards the ferry building where a car was waiting. A woman got out and helped him into the front seat. She stowed the frame in the boot, straightened up, and looked around. Her eyes rested a moment on Maurice. It was Laura. Maurice smiled and half stood, but she turned away, seeming not to have recognized him.

114

Had he changed so much? Or was it just that she didn't want to acknowledge, or to remember, what friends they had been? Maurice felt it – a disappointment, almost a hurt. Ginny had told him she was baby-sitter for Laura and her husband Roger Barber, and that she liked the husband but not the wife.

Laura was getting into the car now. Maurice could see her talking to her father, doing up his seat-belt. In a moment the car was cruising away into the traffic.

He got up and walked down towards where the liner had docked; then to the fishing boat moorings at the Western Viaduct. The boats were coming in under the raised road-bridge, tying up, unloading their catch.

He'd told Ginny that his life had been given over to a mistake. It was true, wasn't it? What was Marxism if it wasn't economics, and as economics it had failed. As a system of government it had been a disaster – a tragedy.

But for him it had also been an ideal. It had been comradeship, and goodwill, and earnest endeavour, and adventure. Why should he care about always being right? Any fool could be that! In old age it was the things not done that you regretted, more – far more – than the mistakes.

Laura. There was the time he'd taken her to see the stream in the bush on what had been his father's farm . . .

Maurice's mind shifted a gear into something that was as vivid as a dream. He was a boy again, taking a short cut over the sill of an open sash window, out on to the verandah where his gumboots, the smallest pair, were lined up with all the others. He sat on the step and pulled them on; he went out past the manuka brush fence that sheltered the vegetable garden, over the big gate and down the line of blue gums; down the slope and across the swampy hollow where cows' hoofs made neat, deep cloven shafts; through manuka scrub and on into the part of the farm that had never been "brought in" from bush and which his father told them they should consider sacred, never to be felled. Now he was making his way over the brown, dry littered ground strewn with mossy logs and grey dropped branches and bronzy fallen kauri foliage in the filtered light, until he came to his favourite place under a high enclosing roof of trees and sat watching shafts of light striking into a broad, still pool below a little waterfall.

Maurice sat there in his mind. He saw himself and was himself. He saw his boy's brown knees, his gumboots, his khaki shorts, his green shirt, his tousled hair and freckles, his keen eyes and eager pointed face. That's me, he thought. My real self. Everything else comes after, added on. When that boy goes, everything goes. The great Nothing will meet me, face to face.

*     *     *

Dan's visit is over. They've talked about his aunt's cottage. Laura has remembered that today is his birthday. He has left "The Magic Bagwash" for her to read; and kissed her at the door.

Out in the street his driver is waiting. Dan directs him to a little bay he remembers from long ago, gets out and walks down to the sand. The coast curves here and he can see across the water to the larger beach where he grew up. A kilometre away he can pick out the wooden fence and the pines where he played as a child, and the upper windows of the house.

It's a calm day – no waves, not even a faint swell – and he has that sensation peculiar to the Hauraki Gulf of a level plain of water, an expanse, beginning at his feet, stretching away to Rangitoto and the other islands, and to that wide gap through which shipping passes out into open ocean – so calm compared to the west coast, sheltered by islands and by the Coromandel peninsula, yet also in its own way generous, open, vast and, to Dan, incomparably beautiful.

He remembers sailing out there with his uncle and others in a yacht, a "50 foot A-class keeler" (that description impressed him) and the sensation of quietly swishing and skimming under cliffs and past pohutukawa-shaded bays. There are yachts out there now, stalled on the windless water. Right on the horizon a container ship sits square and high and stationary, waiting for the call from port.

He walks up the road from the beach to a headland, formerly a military camp, now a park, with big gun emplacements that once guarded the passage to and from the harbour. The park runs out to the cliff edge. A wooden stairway goes almost vertically, through undergrowth, down the cliff face, then turns and goes out of sight. He goes as far as the turning, sees the beach below, and continues until he comes to the sand, shut off by rocks at either end. And now he remembers his Aunt Amelia brought him here when he was a boy. Not alone – with a man, possibly one of her writer friends. Could it have been Maurice Scobie? They climbed down to swim below the cliffs, and the friend, in his bathing suit, found a stick he pretended was a musical pipe, and with seaweed wreathed in his hair did a Pan-dance in the shallows, prancing on his toes, lifting his knees high, bending forward as if playing on the pipe. And just at that moment the big guns up on the headland went off – a practice firing, or perhaps a salute, that caused Aunt Amelia to shriek and the dancer to drop his Pan pipe.

In Dan's pocket is a key to the cottage. He intends, one day before it's sold, to take a last look. He remembers visiting it as a child, a place stacked with books and littered with manuscripts, but orderly, its walls lined with a kind of Polynesian matting.

Now it occurs to him that Laura won't ever have seen

117

inside it. He could take her there – and why should he not go back and suggest it now? His absence from the lunch he's in Auckland to attend will be noticed; but does it matter?

He stands, as if waiting to see what he will do. The sea makes a small flapping sound as it advances up the sand, and a small sigh as it draws back. The stalled yachts out there seem to pick up a faint breath. Sunlight glitters on the water.

# FIVE

# 1970/1990 – Lies or Madness

My typescript has a red cover held together by metal clips that are tinged with rust. The name "Laura Jackson" is inked across the top, the "Jackson" crossed out and replaced by "Barber".

I cross out the "Barber" and write "Ingalls Wilder".

Delay, evasion, cowardice, funk.

I decide I won't read it. Won't because I can't. Then that I can and will. Ten years is long enough. What am I afraid of? Insincerity? Bad prose? That the past, after so long, might condemn the present? That it might be dead? If I don't like what I find I can put it away – or burn it. There has to be something I can learn from it.

I let the pages fan through my fingers, rediscovering the names I gave my characters. Dave Carter – that's Dan, of course. Roger is Larry and I'm Larissa Vincent. My father is Jack. Caroline – my friend, my flat-mate, my companion, my competitor – is simply Caroline. Is there, was there, in that failure to change her name, an author's insight, a foreboding? Or is the change random, and do right things happen only by chance?

Hold my hand, Hildamelia.

I select a scene at random, and read. There! Painless. I read it again – not with pleasure or satisfaction, but without distress.

It takes place at night. Larissa and Dave arrive outside the little wooden two-storeyed house in Grafton. There's a description of the house, the overgrown garden at the front, the wilderness of trees at the back, the coloured glass door panes, the wooden lattice work around the verandah.

They're talking about the night they first met. She doesn't tell him that she came down to the court that night, not really to practice her serve, but because she wanted to meet him. She tells him only that she'd heard of him and read an interview with him in *Craccum* which referred to him as a pacifist.

He says pacifist was their word, not his. A pacifist opposes all wars.

"And you choose, do you?" she says.

He smiles. Then he laughs. Then he kisses her.

He tells her the house looks like a cuckoo clock. The cuckoo should come out of the attic window – her bedroom, in the angle under the eaves.

They get out of the car. There's a big round moon coming up over the trees of the Domain. He tells her to close her eyes, takes her by the shoulders, steers her, and says, "OK. Look at your roof spike." The yellow moon-ball is sitting exactly on the point of the finial. The scene concludes:

"She turned to him. 'Cuckoo clocks and spiked moons', she said. It was like a question. All around the house the pale light glittered on leaves, and the house itself stood up tall and thin, white and unreal."

★　　★　　★

Larissa waking. She drew one foot up and stretched the other down to the bottom of the bed, running her hands over her body as if it belonged to someone else, remembering Dave showing her the moon balancing on the spike over her window. The day was already warm. The hum of traffic came up from the street. Light wavered on the ceiling. Downstairs, Caroline was banging about – early and virtuous, Larissa thought, and asserting herself.

She got out of bed and looked at herself in the mirror.

Through her thin nightdress she could see her nipples and the shadow of her pubic hair. She pulled the nightdress up to her chin and looked at her naked body, moved her hips, then threw it off and went to the bathroom.

As she turned off the shower, she could hear Caroline calling up to ask whether she was awake.

"Just drying myself," she shouted.

"Well, don't hurry or anything", Caroline called, "but I've cooked the bacon."

Down in the kitchen Caroline was reading the *Herald*. Larissa's place was set, her glass of orange juice poured, her bread ready in the toaster. Caroline's dishes were cleared away. On the gas stove in a thin, buckled, blackened frying pan three curly rashers of bacon lay in fat which was just losing its transparency.

Caroline didn't look up.

OK, Larissa thought, so she's worked herself up. That can be dealt with; and she swept around the table and gave her flat-mate a hug. "I'm sorry. Late again – and you've done it all."

Caroline's look – deliberately blank – couldn't hide it: she liked this kind of fuss. Needed it. But at the same time as Larissa gave generously, she wanted to take it away – to tease, to exercise the power she felt was hers. So she said, "I think I'll have an egg too. Any eggs?"

"There might be one."

"Only one?"

"Have it."

"What about your lunch?"

Caroline shrugged. "I'll find something."

"Sure now?"

"Quite sure."

As she broke it into the pan Larissa thought, It takes character to eat the last egg.

"You know if we really lived perfectly," she said, bringing her plate to the table; "I mean if we got the most out of everything, breakfast could be a kind of Zen. It might take all day."

"You're getting there," Caroline said.

Larissa looked up from her toast. Was the worm turning? "I could do better. But don't take that as a threat, dearest." She shook the pot. "Care for some weedkiller tea?"

Caroline held out her cup. "Larry didn't come in last night."

"Oh . . . No, he didn't." She laughed, and stopped herself because it sounded artificial. "Sorry. That's what used to be called 'a gay little laugh'. In fact it wasn't Larry brought me home. It was Dave."

Caroline stared. "Dave Carter? Anarchist Dave?"

"The same."

"Why?"

"Why?" Larissa thought about it. An honest answer wouldn't please Caroline, so she gave it. "I think he's in love with me."

"But I thought you and Larry . . ." They stared at one another. "I mean, isn't it – *inconvenient*?"

"I hadn't thought of it as – inconvenient." She laughed. "What a funny word. I suppose it might be inconvenient for Dave."

*       *       *

Rain. I sit at my work table, the red-covered typescript open, and look out at the sea and the islands fading into a watery wash. Angled columns march over like an invading army. All that's clear now is the immediate suburb, the houses descending to the sea front. Big beautiful clear drops hit the roof next door, not breaking immediately but bouncing, catching the light. Drops run like ski-lifts down the wires from the street to the house.

Angela calls from her bedroom. She's home from school

with a cold – no more than an excuse to stay in bed and read *Little House on the Prairie*. She wants to know what I'm doing, and I tell her I'm reading something I wrote a long time ago – a story.

She didn't know I wrote stories. "Is it good?" she wants to know.

I tell her I don't think so. "But it's interesting. Interesting to me."

I wrote it before she was born. Now that the seal has been broken I go back to it often – not as something that might be rescued, revised, published. Whether it's "good" is not much on my mind. It belongs to a past self, a past age.

But I can see how I must have worked at it, trying to get away from myself – my Larissa self – and inside Dan's experience, and Roger's. There's a scene, for example, between Dave Carter and a character I called Eva, modelled on Dan's friend Kiev.

Fact? Fiction? No, I'm not sure where the line between them lies. Only, let's say, that it was fiction in the service of what had once been fact.

*　　*　　*

Yes, it was summer in Parnell too, and summer all over the gullies and cones of Auckland, and Dave Carter sat cross-legged, naked on Eva's bed, one hand on her bare thigh, deliberately putting out of his mind all thought of Vietnam, and the essay he was writing about the war there, and what his friends thought of the essay, concentrating instead on a blow-fly that was zooming in and out of sunlight through the open window, with a swerving flight-path and a speed that would have made you anxious for its safety if you didn't know that when they did crash – into a window pane for example – those little machines hardly faltered, they just bounced, fell stunned to the floor, buzzed around on their backs in three or four circles and figures of eight, and then took off again at the same mad speed.

Zoom again. It had only one gear. Zoom – out and away across the grass to the hedge, left around the grapefruit tree and out of sight, and there was a moment of something like silence before you heard it again, making a low run now over Eva's belly, up past the big torn triangle of green wallpaper and across the brown ceiling with footprints in white paint running across it.

Silence. Too sudden. It hadn't gone this time, had stopped, alighted on something. Where? Not . . . No – there, look, in a shaft of light on the pile of clothes Eva had shed on the floor. The blow-fly reflective. Appreciative . . .

Zoom – away past the Toulouse-Lautrec poster and out into the garden . . .

This summer the blow-flies were bigger than usual, and there were more. Mosquitoes too, and cicadas. But house flies had disappeared. Jack Vincent said it was because the grass wasn't growing and there wasn't moist humus for them to breed in.

Zoom. It was back, but this time it was gone as quickly, straight into the passage. Let it find the kitchen. No – let it not find the kitchen, in which Eva . . .

Eva. Half asleep. Delicate curve of eyebrow, aquiline nose, cheeks firm and lightly freckled, shoulders small and white and round (vulnerable, they seemed, when she turned on her stomach), breasts large with small, pink, unassertive nipples, belly rounded as if she had borne children, pubic hair wispy, good legs . . .

Dave had first seen her like that – it must have been five years ago. And all at once, remembering, he was smitten with nostalgia for the time when he'd said goodbye to his mother, and to his aunt with her telescope and her starched tea-cloths, goodbye to the pines and the board fence and the orange sand and the view of Rangitoto, goodbye to the tennis club and to the Law. How had he managed it?

Don't think. Be. He needed a mantra. He needed the blow-fly to hold his attention but it was silent, gone, and he imagined it laying its tiny white cluster of eggs in a fatty corner of a piece of cold corned beef with a purple shine to it that Eva might have left on the kitchen table.

He closed his eyes. He felt a longing – for what? Maybe this was nothing more than the post-coital sadness he'd thought occurred only in books. Eva was beyond him, away in her own dream, glad to have him as her lover – one of her lovers.

Om. Mani. Padme. Hum. You're here. You are. Your hand is squeezing Eva's thigh. The blow-fly is ecstatically laying down a future in cold corned beef.

She opened her eyes. They were round and blue, not quite awake. They took him in passively and closed again. He wasn't in love with her. Hadn't ever been. What did that mean? Staring down at her he felt affection, gratitude, a sort of indifference that was a sort of love and which otherwise might have been despair, because in some sense Eva was never there. She was away on a cloud. Was it drugs, or temperament? He didn't know. But she was a wonderful fuck.

She yawned, a yawn that got bigger and turned into a gasp. It woke her. "From here, Dave Carter," she said, "you have a determined mouth."

"You know why, don't you? It's because I have a weak character. In the right war I might have won a medal. To prove myself."

"I'd give you a medal."

"Jack Vincent told me another of his war stories last night. You know what I felt? Envy."

"You should have blocked your ears."

He laughed at that, and sat back thinking about Jack with his iron haircut, his RSA badge and his bullish opinions. "I like him. I listen to him. Why is that?"

"He must be a nice man."

Dave stared at her. She always surprised him. "You have a beautiful soul, Eva."

"Are you going to make me a cup of coffee?"

"And he's got a daughter – Larissa."

"The tennis player. You told me."

"What would you think if I said I was going to marry her?"

"Why does anyone get married? It's so final."

"I'm not getting married. I just said supposing I told you I was going to."

"Well, if you're not, it wouldn't be true."

"Yes, but . . ." He got out of bed and pulled on his underpants. "You're so literal, Eva. Can't you imagine something?"

"Of course I can. But not that."

He went over to the window and stared into the garden. He was reluctant to go and make coffee because he knew when you walked barefoot into that kitchen you felt crumbs and sugar and sticky patches that might have been jam or spilled milk. Orts, Manning Strettor called them when he visited. He made a joke of it, but it was obvious he didn't like orts any more than Dave did. Dave tried to hide his distaste. It wasn't his house. And his desire for cleanliness and order – wasn't that just part of his bourgeois hangup? Om. Mani. Padme Hum. Peace, brother.

He turned from the window. Still naked, Eva was lying with one arm behind her head, one leg just slightly bent, and the foot of the other tucked behind her knee. Matisse-style. Reclining odalisque. Eyes closed. Expression something like petulance, something like stupidity – but it was neither. She was awake and he could read her. She knew he would turn from the window and see her like that. She didn't want coffee now. She wanted him.

He went across to the bed and sat down at its edge and put the heel of his hand between her legs, pressing gently up into her, then more firmly, spreading his fingers through her pubic hair. She put her hand over his, increasing the pressure.

Dave said, "Have you ever seen a bull and a cow when the cow's on heat and they've been penned together for hours?"

She shook her head, eyes closed, moving his hand against her, round in a slow circle.

"The cow rests her chin on the railing and looks at the hills and the bull stands with his nose in her arse and a mad dreamy spring-flowers look in his eyes, and every now and then he moves his head sideways as if he's got a stiff neck and he goes Mmmmmm-*mmmmmmhh*. Mmmmmm-*mmmmmmhhhh*." As he imitated the bull-sound Dave pressed in harder with the heel of his hand. "It's the noise he makes when he bellows, only with the volume turned right down. He's thinking he'd like to, but he doesn't know whether he can – he's done it too often. And then he thinks he will – he'll give it a shot. And he heaves himself up. It's an effort. She staggers under the weight. But now she's got that spring-flowers look too, and he's pumping away . . ."

Still with her eyes closed Eva felt for his underpants and gave them a tug. "Get them off, Mr Bull."

Suddenly the room was full of sound. A cicada had lighted on the window frame in the sun. Dave threw his underpants at it and it fell with them out into the garden.

*　　*　　*

A knock at the back door: it was Ginny Scobie in running gear. Rain almost gone, but the sky overcast – low misty webs still drifting in from the sea, fine drops of it in the hair of this wet-weather Aphrodite, long-legged, shining-limbed, stopping by to report progress with the petition (Roger's doing) to support the Tapler purchase. There were several hundred more signatures. She would have the sheets assembled by tomorrow.

So come in, Spinner. She protested she was wet, would make puddles on the floor, but in she came, and sat at the kitchen table, everything about her soft and clear. An effect of light? Of moist air? Or because I usually saw her at night, properly dressed and with makeup? She was young, and beautiful. If I'd been a man I would have found her . . . God yes!

Young/beautiful: Not synonyms, no. But I'd reached an age when they weren't entirely separable. I felt a twinge, not of jealousy exactly, more like fear – but it wasn't simple. It was also excitement. This was my younger self – my Larissa-self. Young men were strong, but they were blunderers. They barged about and trampled things down, but they played by a set of rules. Young women were the anarchists.

Making conversation – not easy with Ginny (or not for me) – I told her I'd been reading over something written years before; a novel, never finished.

"That's interesting," she said – a sure sign that it wasn't – so I told her Maurice figured in it; that I'd called him Manning Strettor. "Same initials, but suitably patrician, don't you think? There was always something so civilized about Maurice. He represented the intellectual Left."

"He doesn't change," she said. "A poem for every occasion."

I told her I thought I'd seen him down at the waterfront one day, but hadn't realized until too late who it was.

This wasn't true. That rugged face – I'd been surprised that it had seemed both so old and so instantly familiar.

Even in fiction I hadn't been able to deal with Maurice . . . "Manning Strettor". It was as if I'd bought off his memory with a fancy name, and left it at that.

"He's well, is he?" I asked.

Ginny said she thought so. "He's getting on, of course." Her expression, as she said it, was enquiring. Almost defensive. "He's my favourite rel," she said. "I love him."

I gave her a sympathetic look. "That's understandable. I loved him once."

I wondered was that true? Or had I said it for effect? But it was a statement from which either advance or retreat would have been a mistake, so I busied myself with the coffee.

Ginny's eyes followed me. "He must have . . ." she said, and then hesitated. "You must have been a lot . . . There would have been quite a difference . . ."

A delicate subject?

I said, "You mean in age? Yes. Quite a difference. At first I thought of him as old. Then I didn't think about age at all. It was irrelevant."

She stared into her cup. I felt I was being carried along by something I couldn't quite control. I meant to talk about the petition, but found myself saying, "Young women respond to older men, don't they?"

Ginny's face reddened slightly. "I suppose so," she said. "It depends on the older man."

"And on the younger woman," I said.

When she was gone I went back to my table. I didn't want to think about her. She distracted me from my work. I meant to get on with Hilda's manuscripts, but opened the red-covered typescript for a moment, more or less at random. There was a scene . . .

Larissa has prepared a special meal for Larry. There are candles, wine, flowers on the table, windows open to the gully. In the kitchen something special is cooking in an enamel casserole. On the record player is the Joni Mitchell album, "Clouds", with the title track they listened to the first night they spent together. The memory of it comes back to Larissa with that shimmering atmosphere of moon-light on leaves below an open window. But the words of the song, when she croons them to herself, are cleverer than the romance of it, and less reassuring:

I've looked at love from both sides now,
From win and lose, and still, somehow,
It's love's illusions I recall.
I really don't know love at all.


And so on . . .

And "somehow" (as the song says) the dinner party for two went horribly wrong. Larissa said bitchy things. Larry became jealous and petty. They quarrelled, and he marched out. She was left crying in her chair, the room darkening, the two thin candles tall and elegant but still unlit, and from the kitchen the smell of the beautiful "rice thing" she'd prepared, sticking to the enamel and beginning to burn . . .

I put the typescript down. I remembered this scene, but only faintly; and now I couldn't be sure whether it came back to me as something that had happened, or only as something written. I thought of one of Hilda Tapler's notes suggesting that fiction which was supposed to deal with your own experience had the effect of replacing it. What you wrote became your memory.

But then, Hilda had gone on to ask herself, wasn't all memory just that – a composition (a recomposing) of fact? An ordering into narrative? Everything we said about ourselves, whether inwardly or to others, became a story; and all stories were artificial. But without them the mind would be reduced to the chaos of unordered impressions. Our choice, she'd concluded, was either lies or madness.

Then she'd had second thoughts – accused herself of overstatement; but later added a note saying "Karl Wolfskehl agrees. Refers me to the opening of Nietzsche's *Beyond Good and Evil*."

★　　★　　★

It was only a day or so after Ginny's visit that Maurice rang. He'd talked to Ginny, who had told him of her conversation with me; and this (he explained) had given him the courage to make this call.

"I don't know the best way to put it," he said, "so I'll make it simple and a bit brutal. I've got the big C and I'm on the way out. I've got probably just a few months . . ."

"Oh Maurice, I'm so sorry. I . . ." I felt helpless. What on earth did one say? "Are you sure it can't . . ."

He interrupted. "No no no. No need for that, old girl. It's just that there are half a dozen people I want to see while I'm still presentable. You're one of them, Laura. A brief visit, if you could make it."

His voice was familiar, firm, hardly changed. I said, "Of course I'll come."

"It's a bit like a royal command, isn't it? A dying man's wish and all that. I haven't told Ginny yet, so please . . ."

"I won't mention it."

For a moment I stopped listening, trying to take in what he'd told me. Then I realized he was talking about a terrible crime that had just gone to trial – the murder of a young mother by a teenage burglar. The details were horrible, and I didn't know how he meant me to respond.

"That's not the only one," he said. "There's Tamihere and the Swedes . . ."

"Oh yes," I said. "Awful. Ghastly."

"And the boy who tried to behead the judge with a machete. Said he wanted to put her out of her misery." There was a pause. "That's a bit different . . . Quite funny, really."

What was he trying to say? I said, "Maurice, I've missed something here . . ."

He was embarrassed. "Oh God, sorry. Not making much sense." And then he tried to explain. "It's just that – well, you see I've noticed when old people start to fall to pieces they think *everything* is. So I think probably I'm

131

letting myself become obsessed, because . . . You see?"

I made a stab at what seemed an appropriate response. "You want me to say everything's OK?"

He laughed. "No wonder I loved you Laura. Yes, please – if you wouldn't mind."

So I said it. "Everything's OK, Maurice. We've just had a few more rumpuses than usual lately."

"Thanks. That's my woman."

"And Maurice . . ."

"Yes?"

"You didn't love me."

"Didn't I? Well, I won't argue with you. But my God I liked you a lot. What a backhand!"

I said I would see him next week. "And stop reading the crime pages," I told him. "Just because you can't face the politics . . ."

"Bye, sweetheart." He was laughing now. "You've made an old man's day."

But when I left the phone I was dismayed. There were the details of those murders, which if you let your mind linger on them might indeed begin to haunt you. And nearer, less abstract, the news that Maurice was going to die. The fact sank in. It sank deeper. I sat in a chair and thought about him until the tears came. Of course it had to happen. He was old. But how old? And whether it had to happen or not had nothing to do with my feelings about it. How could I have turned away from him like that, down at the waterfront? There was my father too. But Vince was recovering, whereas Maurice had said for him it was only a matter of months.

I went to my typescript and began to hunt for him but he wasn't there. There was only that invented name, Manning Strettor, with nothing attached to it except the mention of him as a visitor to the house in Parnell. Roger, too, had vanished. He'd marched out of that disastrous dinner for two, taking the name Larry out of my story; and at the point where I'd given up, he still hadn't returned. So it had threatened to turn into a novel about Larissa and Dave.

No wonder I'd given it up!

\* \* \*

The sun was beating down on Dave's car. He wound the windows down. From the gully the sound of bulldozers drifted up, and behind it the more regular hum of cars on the finished strip of motorway. The air was dusty. There was a haze over the city. Dave stared up at the little house he had once said looked like a cuckoo clock. The curtains were drawn over the upper window. A moment ago he'd hammered on the door and there had been no reply. He ought to drive away but he couldn't quite rid himself of the conviction that Larissa was there. And if she was, why didn't she answer? She had been strangely distant these past weeks – since that awful day out at the coast when she had almost drowned.

Might there be someone with her now? Larry, for example? Dave felt sick and anxious. He had peered through the downstairs windows. Everything looked normal, untidy but orderly. The milk had been taken in. There were three letters in the box. On the line at the back there was some washing – underwear, shirts, tea-towels, jeans. The back door was locked.

He got out and returned to the front door, rattled it, stood back and called Larissa's name.

At the back of the house he tried the windows that opened off the verandah. One was unlocked and he pushed it up.

"Anyone home?" he called, putting his foot over the sill. "Hullo there, Larissa. Caroline. It's Dave. I'm coming up."

The steep little stairway shone with white enamel. Halfway up he stopped for a moment and leaned against the wall. At the top he found the bedroom door ajar. He pushed it open.

133

Larissa was in bed asleep, face down, her head turned to the wall. He could see the faint movement of her back and shoulders as she breathed. He went to the window and looked out. Three white doves were perched on the roof of the house next door. One slid and scrambled on the roof slope and then took off, followed by the others, their wings clattering like a round of applause as they swept out in a wide circle. He felt at that moment so fortunate, they seemed like omens, and when they were out of sight he couldn't quite believe he'd seen them.

He sat down in a wicker chair. Looking at her soft ruffled hair, pale neck, smooth brown shoulders, he felt an over-whelming tenderness. After a time he got up and walked about the room. The closet was half open and he ran a hand over the clothes, evoking her by textures and scents. There were papers scattered over her desk, lecture notes, passages copied out of books, a letter from a friend, a half-written essay about Shelley with a quotation beginning

Emily,
A ship is floating in the harbour now,
A wind is hovering o'er the mountain's brow;
There is a path on the sea's azure floor,
No keel has ever ploughed that path before . . .

He returned to the chair and thought of the sea's azure floor, and his uncle sailing out over it, watched by his aunt's telescope, out through that wide blue gap between Rangi-toto and the Whangaparaoa Peninsula, until the ship seemed to sit up high on the very edge of the world, and finally to slide over it.

Larissa had moved in her sleep. He could see her face in profile, slightly distorted by the downward pressure. He wanted to touch her, wanted to take off his clothes and get into bed with her.

When she woke and looked at him her eyes were lifeless

at first. "How did you get in?" she murmured. She turned over, drawing the sheet up to her shoulder.

He put his hand on her thigh. "Sleeping late?"

"Mm."

"Something the matter?"

"Mm."

"Want to tell me about it?"

"No."

Her face was turned away and he thought she might be crying. Suddenly she threw the covers back and went straight to the bathroom without speaking. She was in there a long time.

When she came out she was gleamingly naked, her nipples standing out, her pubic hair shiny, catching the light, curling like symbolic waves. Still she didn't speak but went to her chest of drawers, taking out underpants and bra, then to the closet, selecting a shirt and skirt, jacket and shoes.

His disappointment was so acute it made him angry, conscious of how much he wanted to be with her in that big bed they called "the playing field". Yet something – pride, or the prohibition which her silence communicated – wouldn't allow him to say it. For a moment he thought of raping her, not as something he might do, but as something his imagination could take refuge in.

In a quiet voice that sounded menacing even to himself he asked, "Are you going to tell me what's happening?"

She looked at him and there was a flinch of sympathetic pain in her face. He thought that some barrier was about to fall and that she would rush at him and tell me that she loved him. But the moment passed. She looked around the room, found her purse and her hair brush, pushed them into the pocket of her suede jacket, hooked the strap of a little woven bag over her shoulder, and walked to the door where she turned and looked back at him.

"What's happening," she said, "is . . . *nothing*. Nothing

is happening. I'm having a – an *episode*. You understand?"

No, he didn't understand. But as she stood there, hesitant, he had the feeling that whatever she was doing, wherever she was going, it involved an act of will, a violence, which she half hoped he would prevent. It needed only an opposing violence to break the barrier between them; but he lacked the courage, or the confidence, and he thought she would probably blame him for that – hold it against him as a failure.

She was halfway out of the door now, but again she turned back. "You want sex," she said. "Try Caroline. She's been wanting to suck your cock all term. She'll be back at ten, after her lecture."

She turned and walked down the stairs. He heard the front door open and shut again. He went to the window, saw her walk down the path and out of the gate, cross the street determinedly, almost angrily, through traffic, as if it had no right to be there. Soon she turned the corner and was gone.

He pushed up the sash and leaned his elbows on the sill. His stomach was twisted in a knot of anxiety. He thought, "This is the worst day of my life."

The three doves clattered down on the roof again, and one, the biggest, its neck puffed out, walked up and down the ridge, nodding its head and making a long, repetitive warbling pigeon speech.

Before long he saw Caroline coming down the street.

★     ★     ★

Lies or madness. Beyond good and evil. Nietsche red in tooth and claw. Whether or not it was lies, it certainly seemed like madness. I knew now why I had kept the red covers shut, and the cupboard door shut on the red covers. Laura should have stuck to Ingalls Wilder and the little house on the prairie, with a story-curl of story-smoke going up into a story-sky. But I wasn't going to stop now. I read on.

What should have followed was my trip north with Maurice. That was where I had gone that day, after walking out on Dan. Or rather, since I'm no longer sure what is the truth: that was where Larissa went after walking out on Dave. But the pages, which had certainly been written, were gone; and in some dim head-corner or mind-recess there was a cobwebby recollection of having burned them. In the next section Larissa was already in Northland. How she had got there wasn't told. It was getting on towards evening and she was sitting alone in a cream stand at the roadside, watching two horses in a paddock.

★　　★　　★

They were a chestnut horse and a grey, and there was something odd about the way they were behaving. The chestnut stayed in one place, but tossed its head as if distressed. The grey circled it, breaking into a trot, slowing, snorting, changing direction.

Then, as Larissa watched, the stationary horse seemed to quiver, its body shook for a moment, and it fell – simply keeled over and disappeared in the long grass, while the other circled faster, tossing and whinnying.

She jumped down from the cream stand, crossed the road, scrambled through a fence, and ran to the horses. The one that was down lifted its head, its eye bulging, the veins on its neck standing out, its skin sweating. She could see now – there was a loop of wire attached to an old post. It went round the hind legs. The horse had got tangled, had gone around in circles binding itself tighter, until now the legs were held together, the skin broken, the flesh raw, white and red.

She tried to loosen the wire but her hands weren't strong enough. She stood up and saw a small, unpainted wooden

137

bungalow among trees at the top of the slope. She ran to it and was met by a Maori man who came out on to the verandah. Breathless, she told him what she'd seen. He came down the steps, went back indoors, returned with a file.

"Show me," he said.

When they reached the horses nothing had changed. Larissa held the hooves clear of the ground while the man worked with the file. It was fencing wire and he struggled with it, spitting to cool it while he worked. The horse lay still, its hooves, huge and heavy, cupped in Larissa's hands.

When the legs were freed the man coaxed the horse to stand. It struggled up, hobbling.

"Needs the vet, eh?" he said.

Now he and Larissa were able to talk. He asked her how she came to be on this lonely road and she told him she'd been hitch-hiking; then walked a few miles since her last lift. She'd been expecting to find the coast. Her last driver had told her she would find a motel and a store there, but she hadn't come to it.

"Here," the Maori said. "Look." He guided her a short way up the slope, pointed her in the right direction. In the intersection of two downward slopes the blue ceased to be sky. It crossed a smudge of cloud, a faint immaculate line, and became a brief glimpse, a gleaming reach, of sea.

The sun had gone behind hills and now the sky was pale and immense. In the fields spiky things stood out – fence posts, clusters of rushes and flax, clumps of manuka and of gorse. The horses had climbed a small hill and were standing together, motionless, silhouetted.

"It's getting dark," she said. "I'd better be on my way."

"Yeah, OK. Well – thanks for coming to get me. Lucky for us you noticed, eh?"

"Lucky for the horse." She was affected by his shyness. "Goodbye." She held out her hand. "This is all round the wrong way, but I'm Larissa."

"Hey, Larissa." His voice hummed it out in a tone that seemed to say, What a nice name! "I'm Hone."

"Nice to meet you, Hone."

"You all fixed up for kai?"

"Well – I thought down on the coast . . . To tell the embarrassing truth, I'm a bit lost."

"You should've said, Larissa. You wouldn't like to . . . ah . . . Plenty kai up at the house. Wife and kids . . ." His voice trailed away.

"If it's no trouble that would be . . ." They were smiling at one another. "I haven't eaten since breakfast," she said.

He whistled his surprise. "Let's go. Up there's a big roast."

"I know. I could smell it when I came to get you."

They walked together back towards the house through the darkening fields.

\*       \*       \*

That was all. End of folder – oh, except for a handwritten note to myself worrying about the fact that I didn't seem able to control the story, that it was getting away from me, and from "the truth" (what was that?). And resolving to "put it aside for a while and come back to it fresh".

Then or later I must have destroyed the pages about Maurice, about the visit I made with him to his childhood farm. No loss in itself. But now Maurice was dying . . .

\*       \*       \*

I remember little of the early part of the drive, except that it began in depression and guilt, because I'd treated Dan so badly; and then that excitement began to take over as we got away from Auckland, a feeling of relief because I was clearing out, leaving it all behind, saying to hell with everything; and also because in my imagination since childhood "up north" meant a place where summer never quite went away. It meant warm, still, green estuaries, and small fish around wooden wharf piles swimming to stay in one place against the running tide; and big fish, kahawai or kingies, going through them like harvesters, sending them sprinting to left and right. It meant mangrove swamps, shell-fish, hangis, brown faces, white sands, giant kauris. It meant the Treaty House too, and the little weatherboard town of Russell across the water from Paihea, where Hone Heke had three times cut down the flag-pole.

At first we hardly talked at all; and then when we got to a place called Kaiwaka Maurice began to tell me about it as it had been in the 1920s. He described a dusty crossroads, a bridge over a stream, a country store, a post office and telephone exchange, a tiny wooden church, and a one-room wooden schoolhouse with the children's ponies grazing in a paddock. That was all, where now there were the beginnings of a town.

We drove down the back road Maurice had travelled on horseback to and from school. It still wasn't sealed, and he knew every turn of it, every fold in the fields on either side, every creek and swamp and patch of bush.

His monologue seemed impersonal, addressed to no one in particular. He was so intent, so lost in what was out there, it made me feel privileged – and foolish. I think I'd imagined holding him at arm's length and now here I was wanting to attract his attention, have him notice me.

Somewhere along that road we turned in through an old five-barred gate and drove across fields, following a rutted track formed years earlier by the horse-drawn sledge that took cream cans from the milking shed to the gate.

We came to a garden gate, parked the car, and went in. The garden and house, long since abandoned in favour of a new house nearer the road, were almost completely enclosed by trees, macrocarpas at one side and at the front, pines at the back, eucalypts along the outer edge of the tennis court. There was still a grassy path, between flower beds, from the gate to the steps up to the front verandah; and the beds, overgrown with weeds, were still full of flowers and flowering shrubs. It was hot in that enclosure, breathless and heavy with scent, humming and buzzing and glinting with insect wings.

Indoors the house wasn't derelict exactly, but neglected. In some of the rooms doors and windows were open to the verandahs that went round on three sides. We disturbed hens that squawked and went half-running half-flying out into the garden. There were saddles and harness on the verandahs, old slashers and gum-spears, axe handles, rabbit traps, a rusty shot-gun. In the kitchen the black wood-range looked serviceable and there was a lantern in the middle of the big scrubbed table. On the wall was an old-style telephone with turning handle and bells for sending signals down the party line.

That afternoon we went for a walk – out over the farm until we came to the bush section which Maurice told me the family had agreed would never be milled, and which contained, more or less at its centre, one giant kauri.

I walked behind him. We were soon deep in the bush and it wasn't long before we came to the stream that was for Maurice what he called, with an irony that didn't conceal his seriousness, one of the holy places. We squatted there watching shafts of light playing on the faintly dusty surface and penetrating it, so the small brown fish which he called kokopu seemed to hang suspended in their element, or to sail through it like aircraft among searchlights. The light was pale, almost white, above the water, and blue within it, like cigarette smoke. There was a small waterfall. Below it the water didn't so much flow as drift, spreading wide and slowing before it narrowed to a rapid again. I could see the shingle bed shading off into dark hollows under the banks where there would be eels.

The waterfall had once descended in two stages. The

banks were steep and moss-covered there, narrowing like a cave entrance, but we managed to scramble up to it. The fall of the water, which must once have come from a great height, had drilled a hole straight down into hard rock, six or seven feet deep and perfectly smooth, just wide enough for one person. The water was clear and perfect, bubbling like champagne as it poured into the dark cup, then sliding out over the lip and down to the pool.

We took turns stripping and lowering ourselves into it. I went first, and then, while I made my way back to the lower bank and dried myself, Maurice followed, sighing and blowing and singing, falsetto, snatches of soprano arias.

That evening we cooked something – sausages and spuds, I think – on the wood range, and sat talking at the big table with the lantern at its centre.

What we talked about I've forgotten, except I remember him telling me that local Maoris wanted to reclaim the bush section because they said his forebear, who first bought it, had swindled theirs.

I asked what he thought, and he said they could go to buggery.

I said it wasn't what he really thought – was it? – and I remember he got up and did a sort of mime, turning the handle of the old wall telephone, lifting the receiver and asking was anyone there. Then he said no, it wasn't what he really thought. But it was what he felt.

Now you have to see us, each in a sleeping bag, on two old brass bedsteads side by side, a faint starlight filling the big sash window, moreporks calling and answering from the bush.

He wanted to know how the daughter of an old Tory like Vince Jackson had come to be Dan Cooper's young woman.

I explained that it was Vince who befriended Dan first and then surprised everyone by inviting him for tennis; and how I'd come down to the court that evening and put on a display of practising my serve, as if I hadn't known who was there.

I must have told how Dan seemed to fall instantly in love, because I remember Maurice laughing and saying "Ace" and "Love forty", and then assuring me he wasn't laughing at Dan. Not at me either. It was the thought of tennis. "Powerful stuff", he called it. "All that leg. And all that beautiful action."

He quoted a poem by John Betjeman about a tennis player called Miss J. Hunter Dunn; and then told me I should read Nabokov's *Lolita*, because there was a scene in which Lolita's besotted abductor, Humbert Humbert, describes her on the court, and goes on about his 'indescribable rapture' watching her play.

But my confession of how I'd come down to the court that night intending to be seen by Dan reminded Maurice of something else – and he told me how he'd first got to know his wife, Ulla. He'd been staying in some sort of Socialist hostel in London after the Spanish War, and one day, sitting out in the quadrangle in the sun, he'd seen the gauze curtain over an open window thrown up and there, for just a moment, was a beautiful female body, naked. He could see her from neck to thighs – her head was above the window and her legs below – and then the gauze floated down and she was hidden. But then up it went again, and floated down – and so it went on. At first he thought it must be someone deranged. Then he remembered how stuffy those rooms were and decided she must be cooling herself. So while he went on watching he was working out which room she was in, and later that day he made some excuse to knock at her door. Everything proceeded from there. After he'd got to know her well he told her what had first attracted his attention, and she pretended to be embarrassed. But years later she told him the truth. She'd overheard him one day talking about Spain, and decided she wanted to get to know him. So yes, she'd been cooling herself; but she'd known he was there under the tree in the courtyard.

Maurice's voice grew quieter as he told this story. He was talking himself into drowsiness. And I remember how, when he came to the end, an unearthly stillness seemed to flow in from the bush and the hills. Even the moreporks seemed to have fallen silent. I lay there feeling that this anecdote, in fact most of his talk that day, had made me anonymous. I was not Laura Jackson; or if I was, I might just as well have been someone else. So what had been the point of all his gallantry and flirting? All I was sure of now was that his motives had been complicated, and that I didn't understand them.

I lay there, wide awake, listening to his breathing – deep, slow and regular, signalling sleep – angry with myself, homesick for Dan.

Next morning, while Maurice whistled and chopped wood for the range, I set out walking until I came to the road. I said nothing to him. He would discover too late that I was gone. But where? The roads up there might veer towards one coast or the other, but ultimately your choice was south or north – towards Auckland or away from it.

I decided I would let fate choose. I waved at every vehicle that came along (there were very few) and the first that stopped for me was a truck heading further north.

That was the day which ended for me with two horses, chestnut and grey, in a lonely field, and with a Maori family's roast pork and puha in a little unpainted bungalow.

\*　　\*　　\*

I've wondered about my memories. Are they safe – or inventions? And then today I put one to the test. I took out John Betjeman's poems from the library and found the two stanzas Maurice quoted to me from the poem about the tennis player.

Miss J. Hunter Dunn, Miss J. Hunter Dunn,
Furnish'd and burnish'd by Aldershot sun,
What strenuous doubles we played after tea,
We in the tournament – you against me!

Love-thirty, love-forty, oh! weakness of joy,
The speed of a swallow, the grace of a boy,
With carefullest carelessness, gaily you won,
I am weak from your loveliness, Joan Hunter Dunn.

Strange, but it gave me a great kick of pleasure to find it, not just because it meant I'd been remembering and not inventing, but also because the lines seemed for a moment like a window into Maurice's mind all that long time ago. I must have seemed so intense, so serious; while for him everything would have been tinged with passionate absurdity, like the poem.

Encouraged by that find I went hunting in *Lolita* and found, though it took much longer, the passage about Humbert Humbert's ecstasy watching Lolita on the court.

★　　　★　　　★

What is to be done with the contents of this red-covered folder of false starts and unfinished stories?

It is fiction (isn't it?) so let fiction dispose of it – as follows:

Saturday morning, overcast, but the rain that has been so heavy during the week seems to have gone over. Laura is out by the garden incinerator. She has a fire going and she's throwing in sheets of typescript, watching the letters darken and persist as each sheet goes black, curling and fading into weak flame. At the same time she's steering Jacob away from it.

Roger comes out into the garden, followed by Ben. He

picks Jacob up so the two-year-old can look down at the fire.

"What's all that?" he asks.

"Some old typescripts of mine."

He leans over to look at a sheaf in her hand but she half turns away. "If I wanted anyone to see it I wouldn't be having a burn-up."

"Secrets?"

"The novel I tried to write when I was pregnant with Angela. Remember?"

He looks as if he has only a hazy recollection. But he's concerned that she should be setting fire to it. "Are you sure you should be doing that?"

She feels her mouth set firm. She is taking in the fact that her shot at novel-writing, which meant so much to her at the time, is something he doesn't clearly recall.

"Quite sure," she says. "I want to get on with my work on Hilda Tapler."

He nods, but his face shows that he doesn't understand – and why should he? A practical man would think the novel, now rediscovered, could be set aside while the thesis was written, and then returned to when it was done. But she isn't going to explain. She can hardly explain these things to herself.

She takes another handful of the sheets and stuffs them down into the flames. She feels the back of her arm prickle as a flame licks momentarily along the fine pale hairs.

Roger is still standing there, irresolute.

"The present's difficult enough," she says, "without trying to cope with the past."

They exchange uncertain smiles.

# SIX

# 1990 – Dog Days

I was busy, and mostly happy, despite anxieties, through those winter months, slowly but surely making discoveries about Hilda Tapler's private life, which I was confident would help to explain her fiction and the way she worked on it. The project to save the Tapler cottage was going ahead, gathering momentum, much less because of anything I was doing than because Roger had thrown himself into the legal side of it, and Ginny Scobie was helping him with petitions. The children were well. Jacob was learning new words every day.

As for the story about Hilda Tapler's meetings with Katya Lawrence – the more I looked at it the more convinced I became that it was true. But I lacked evidence. My belief was based on something that could only be called instinct, or intuition. What Hilda had written about the woman *felt* true; just as the woman's story had *felt* true to Hilda. But how could I say that to Steve? He would answer that my feelings were not a measure of its truth, only of its effectiveness as fiction.

Logically, and in terms of the scholarly disciplines I was supposed to be learning, he was right; but logic and scholarship don't have a monopoly on truth.

One day when we were talking about my work I tried something out on him – less, I suppose, an effort at persuasion than a test of his reaction. "Steve. I want you to listen carefully."

He nodded. "Fire away."

"This is not something out of Hilda's papers. It just comes from my reading about Mansfield. Throughout 1922 – that's the year before she died – Katherine and Murry were drifting away from one another. Their marriage was on the rocks. She went to Paris for treatment, and he only followed reluctantly. Then they went back to Switzerland but they couldn't live together, so they got lodgings in different villages and saw one another at weekends. In August they went to London, but on the second of October Katherine set off for Paris again, leaving him in London. A couple of weeks later she was accepted into the Gurdjieff Institute in Fontainebleau . . . Are you with me?"

"I'm with you."

"Now then. She settles down at the Institute, and then after a time she writes asking Murry to visit her. She suggests either the 8th or 9th of January. He goes on the 9th, and finds her up and about, well and happy. That night she dies."

"Yes?"

"Well, don't you find that even slightly implausible? For more than three months they see absolutely nothing of one another. All reports suggest she's doing better than she has for a long time. Then she nominates a day, he arrives, and she dies."

He grinned. "Murry had a bad effect on people."

"Come on, be serious. I insist. Tell me what you make of that."

He thought for a moment. "I agree it's a long odd. Murry found it rather beautiful, didn't he? I mean, if I have to be honest – it is."

"Beautiful? Steve, who's the sentimentalist here?"

He looked hard at me. "Tell me what *you* make of it."

"I just don't believe it. It's too – *pat*. My point is that this is something that never occurred to Hilda Tapler, but it supports what Katya Lawrence told her . . ."

"If there was a Katya Lawrence. Look, Laura, someone

made all this up. I prefer to think it was Hilda. She was the fiction writer. Katya Lawrence was Hilda's invention."

It was no use going on. Steve's mind was made up; and I had so little apart from hunches to put up against his conviction that the story was fiction – what he called (and this was why it appealed to him) "meta-fiction, ahead of its time".

So what I wrote for him obeyed the scholarly disciplines, acknowledging that the Katya Lawrence story was probably fiction, almost certainly fiction, that it was indeed fiction, while in secret I continued to believe that it was probably/almost certainly/indeed, fact.

I made two visits to the Turnbull Library in Wellington to read letters Hilda had written to other writers whose papers had been deposited there. It was strange to walk past the old Parliament Buildings and the Beehive, knowing that Dan was in there, and on an impulse I phoned his office. I didn't ask to speak to him but just left my name and the phone number of my motel. He called back almost at once. I told him what I was doing, that I was very busy (Back-pedalling? Of course), that I had only a little time in which to read a great deal. He asked wasn't there time at least to call at his office on my way to the library, and it was arranged.

The security guard at the Beehive entrance had my name on a list and gave me a pass. I went up in one of four small lifts to Dan's floor. There were outer offices in which his staff worked and I was funnelled through these to his suite where he sat at a desk with a flag at his back. Opposite was a small bar for ministerial receptions and cocktail parties. At the other end of the room slotted windows looked out to the harbour, and there were comfortable chairs, a couch, coffee tables, a television set – a space where he could relax with visitors or sit in the evening going over papers and waiting for the bells to call him to the Chamber.

I was already worrying about whether I should be making this visit. Did he really welcome an interruption to his day?

And how was I going to explain it to Roger? I decided I would think of it as official, a report on progress at the local end with the Tapler cottage project.

Dan told me he was having trouble with his officials. Opinion polls were running disastrously against Labour and he described himself as a lame duck Minister in a lame duck Government. Things he was keen to see completed were being delayed, while others he felt luke-warm about were pushed at him.

We tried to relax with one another but it wasn't possible. Secretaries were hovering at his open door, and I was conscious of those Tapler letters waiting for me just along the street.

When I said it was time to go he came with me to the lifts. On the way through the outer offices he introduced me to one of his senior officials, Ruth Warner, explaining that I was from Eastern Bays and that Roger and I were part of the group that was hoping to see the Tapler property bought.

Ruth Warner frowned momentarily, as if she wasn't sure what he was talking about. "The Tapler . . . Oh yes." And she shook my hand.

He came down with me in the lift. "She pretends to forget," he said, "to make me aware that it's very low on her list of priorities. Ruth likes to 'prioritize'. And 'diarize'. I'm fighting a small war with her. The Tapler thing's a minor matter. There's money for it. It only needs action by the Department, but she's dragging her feet. I've begun to drag mine on things she wants pushed through Cabinet."

"So will it happen?" I asked.

"Oh, we'll get there," he said.

In the foyer I handed in my security badge. He kissed me on the cheek and I went out into the cool, fresh, clear Wellington air.

★    ★    ★

In her dream Laura gets up from their bed and goes to the window. The garden is clear in the light of a big moon. Dan is looking up at their bedroom; and although he's down on the lawn, she knows he can see her lying in bed with Roger.

The dream frightens her, and she wakes.

Now she does get up and go to the window. There's no moon, none of that inhuman horrible light, bright but obscure, that suffused the dream. But this darkness, shadow and heavier shadow, is sinister too. She can't fight her fear except by waking Roger. He's already stirring.

He stumbles out of bed to the window, peers out, calls. There's nothing, no one.

She begins to tell him what she dreamed. He's getting back into bed, not really wanting to stay awake.

"I know why I dreamed it," she says. "It's because Dan told me that when we were first married he used to stand in our garden and look in at us."

She feels Roger's body jerk with the shock of it. This is something she didn't mean to tell him.

"When did he tell you that?"

"The day he took me to see his aunt's cottage."

"You didn't say he took you there."

She's sure she did – didn't she? Well, she won't argue. Better to explain: "He said while he was in Auckland . . . if we were going to promote the purchase I should see inside the place."

"You didn't tell me you went together."

"Roger, he couldn't leave the key here. He had to keep it. He had to go with me."

Roger grunts. And then, "What kind of creep would look in at windows?"

"It's a long time ago. He was young." She pulls the covers over her. "Let's go to sleep."

Roger sits up. "How the hell do you expect me to go to sleep now?"

"I'm sorry."

"Tell me what happened up there."

"At Hilda's place? What do you mean? Nothing happened. We just had a look around. We talked about the past. I don't know whether it was there or when he called here. He just happened to mention it."

"It's not the kind of confession that pops out in a casual chat, is it?"

"I don't suppose it happened often. He was unhappy about . . . After all . . ."

Roger is out of bed now, pacing, working himself up. She tells him to come back to bed and she'll rub his back.

He says he doesn't want his back rubbed. He wants the truth.

"What truth? Roger, you know the truth. It's not my fault if Dan behaves strangely."

He's beginning to shout. "I've got myself mixed up in this business – petitions, probate, the title – and it turns out to be something you and that failed radical cooked up during an intimate little talk up at the cottage."

"Darling, please. It's no wonder I didn't tell you."

"I thought you said you did."

"Well *if* I didn't . . . Look, nothing happened. Dan came here on his birthday, we talked, we had a cup of coffee, and he left. Twenty minutes later he was back. He said if you and I were going to help, maybe I should take a quick look at the cottage. I can't tell you how much I wanted to get in there. He even let me take away two of her notebooks that hadn't gone to the library."

Silence. He stops pacing.

She tells him she thinks men – not just Dan – all men, are more concerned with the past than women are. It has something to do with ego. Women prefer to live in the present. Men like to walk away, but they don't like to let go. Dan plays irritating games – sends cards, evokes old memories – but Laura is sure he isn't letting the past interfere with his life in the present.

"In fact," she says, "I think he might be having an affair with Caroline. She's down there in Wellington, and divorced. I gather they see a lot of one another."

Roger seems soothed by that. He says he always liked Caroline. He remembers that Maurice called her "palpable" – "a palpable Caroline", like a palpable hit.

Until that moment it hasn't occurred to Laura that Dan and Caroline might be lovers, but the thought has come in the instant of her saying it, and now she's almost convinced it must be true.

She thinks she should probably be pleased for Dan, but whatever she feels, it's not pleasure.

★　　　★　　　★

Aunt Amelia's cottage, Dan told Laura when they went there together, was and was not as he remembered it from childhood. It was quite as picturesque and charming, but smaller. The writer-friend to whom she'd bequeathed it, and whose family now wanted to sell it, had never occupied the place, so it remained just as it had been during Hilda's life. The walls were lined with matting, with books and more books, with paintings and drawings. There were even two notebooks, which, as soon as Laura saw them, she asked to borrow. The windows looked out on a garden overgrown and disorderly, as Dan said it certainly hadn't been in his aunt's younger days; and some of the hibiscus trees had grown tall enough to encroach on that lovely long view out to the bay and the Hauraki Gulf.

Laura was interested to see what Hilda had read. She scanned the shelves and even made a few notes. There was a line of titles by the Italian writer, Alberto Moravia, and Dan told how as a schoolboy he'd been visiting his aunt and had found in her bedroom a novel by Moravia called

*Conjugal Love*, a paperback with a lurid cover. His aunt had come upon him flicking through it. He'd been embarrassed, and thought she would be too, but she'd said "Borrow it. Tell me what you think."

"I accepted. I wanted to read it. But I was a bit shocked – schoolboys are prudes really . . ."

"That she was reading it?"

"Reading it – and suggesting her nephew should."

"But you took it."

"Of course. And it wasn't what the cover had led me to expect. There was sex. But that wasn't what struck me. Really I thought it was the most beautiful book I'd ever read. I suppose I was impressionable – but it was something to do with the style – like a cold, clear light. It gave me a new idea of what a novel could be."

They went into the bedroom and found there the same big bed by the side of which he'd found the copy of *Conjugal Love*. "That was another thing that embarrassed me. Why should an unmarried lady have a double bed? I didn't think she had it to accommodate lovers. But I worried that *other people* might think she did."

"But she did," Laura said. "She had lovers."

"Well," he shrugged. "You're the expert. You know these things. And after all this time, no one's going to be upset by revelations. But in families . . . Or in my family . . ."

Laura was conscious that he was talking partly to cover an unease. He looked at her – there was a kind of appeal; and when she went to move back into the other room, he said it: "I don't know how to cope with you, Laura. I mean with *proximity*. I don't suppose I should tell you what I feel . . ."

"I know what you feel."

"What I want . . ."

"That too."

She was moving away from the bed, towards the door. He reached out and touched her arm. It still made her shiver to have him touch her. "Come on, Dan," she said. "You know that's not possible."

"I don't know unless you say so. It seems perfectly possible to me."

"In my own suburb? With your Government driver waiting out there in the street? You're not . . ."

"It doesn't have to be here and now."

Half an hour earlier, when he'd kissed her at the door of her own house, there had been that moment when she'd wanted him to kick it shut with them both on the inside. Had his impulse come too late? Or was she simply wanting him to force himself on her, so the responsibility would lie with him? As if to remove all doubt she said, "It can't be anywhere, ever."

"Ah, well . . ." He hesitated. "That's different." And then, "At least it's clear."

His acquiescence was so immediate she felt disappointment; but she moved away, and he followed her back into the living room.

He went to the case where his aunt kept her books of poetry and took down the poems of W. B. Yeats. "Listen," he said. "I want to read you something. There's a poem Yeats wrote to open the book he called *Responsibilities*. Do you know it?"

"I don't think so."

"It's an address to his dead ancestors. It begins:

> Pardon, old fathers, if you still remain
> Somewhere in earshot of the story's end . . .

"And then after going through all the things he has to ask their pardon for, it finishes like this:

> Pardon, that for a barren passion's sake,
> Although I have come close on forty-nine
> I have no child, I have nothing but a book,
> Nothing but this to prove your blood and mine."

They looked at one another. He said nothing, waiting for her to respond.

"That was his passion for Maud Gonne," she said. Her own voice sounded faint to her.

"I'm 47," Dan said. "And I don't even have a book."

She felt distressed, confused. Did she have reason to feel guilty? She shook her head and couldn't respond.

"I'm sorry." He was embarrassed now. He put the book back in its place. "I apologize."

"For what?"

"Sentimentality. Emotional blackmail."

"I'm not complaining. I'm touched." It was true; and then she had what seemed at that moment a happy thought – like an escape from responsibility. "Didn't Yeats marry after that? In his fifties? I'm sure he did. He had three children."

"Two," Dan corrected.

When it came time to go and they were walking towards the gate she took his hand and thanked him for bringing her to see the cottage. "It means so much to me, you know, this research. The more I read of your aunt's papers, the more I admire her."

"Good. I'm glad." They stopped and turned towards each other. On what seemed a sudden impulse he asked, "When you ran away from me, up north, did you sleep with Maurice Scobie?"

"By sleep with you mean . . ."

"Fucked."

"No, I didn't." Seeing him looking at her as if the uncertainty remained, she said, "It's such a foolish question."

"Of course. Sophisticated people don't ask."

"I don't care about sophistication. But you're only sure you believe the answer to that question if it's the one you don't want to hear. That's why I never asked it about you and Lee."

"Ask."

She could tell from the way he said it that he was going to profess innocence. So she had her answer; and the same uncertainty about whether it was truthful. "No," she said. "I won't ask. I refuse to consider it. If it ever mattered it certainly doesn't now . . ."

There was a garden seat under a willow. "Here," he said. "Sit down for just a moment and tell me what does matter."

"Between you and me?" She sat beside him, he put an arm round her, and she rested her head on his shoulder. "I should say 'Nothing' – shouldn't I?"

"Say what's true."

"What's true. Heavens! Like 'The world's full of people who regret losing a friend'? It's what all the songs are about, isn't it?"

"I suppose so."

They stayed like that. Once again, Laura thought, they were the lovers on the Grecian urn. There were things they might have said, but they were silent, content to be so close to one another, and surprised to be so at ease.

★    ★    ★

Maurice's letter had no address or date except "My place, Tuesday". It read as follows:

Laurelissima,

Scobie here, love, sitting at my window on the world remembering auld lang syne. Don't mind if I write to you – no need to read now if you're not now inclined; nor ever, if you're never. It has come to me recently that letters are not so much meant for the recipient to receive as for the writer to write.

Speaking of which (writing): I have done myself a memoir and I seem, I, that's to say myself, to have fallen through the cracks. Lots of ideas but no I-deas; no personality. Reading it is like being hit repeatedly with a small plank.

157

So then I thought – *Letters*! I've been firing them off to friend and foe alike – some even far afield, like to, er, um, Amerika (why wasn't she a Russian?) which will be received by the Lady Lee, if at all, with the same profound silence that has greeted all my greetings since those long-ago and erstwhile times.

The luxury of writing letters that have no reason to be writ is that you can make of them what you like. So yours, my dear, will be scones and jam and cream which I recall in your tennis days you ate with abandon (and cream).

Today, for example, I watched, from aforementioned window, young couple moving in next door: he very macho, she very yum. Hatchback parked wrong way about while they unloaded. Later I looked up from book and Oho yes!: car shut but still wrong way about, and curtains closed on windows in front room, presumed bedroom. Good, thinks Scobie: enjoy it while you've got it. "Gather ye rose-buds while ye may/ Old Time is still a-flying/ And that same flower which blooms today/ Tomorrow may be dying . . ." "The grave's a fine and private place/ But none I think do there embrace." Carpe diem. (etc!) BUT. Across the street lives Evil Giant in the form of traffic cop in nasty brown uniform. Out he motors astride his charger, sees car unlawfully parked, pompously prowls checking WOF and registration stickers, takes out pad and – wait for it – *writes a ticket*! Welcome to the suburb!

> Man, proud man!
> Dress'd in a little brief authority.

Scobie watching from his lair is ready to go out and do battle, but being ill and weak thinks better of it. There is another way. So after he'd gone I went down, took the ticket before the newcomers had, so to speak, come. There's an instant fine for which I've instantly written an instant cheque. It will be posted together with this letter to you. Reason: not virtue, not goodness, just *beating the system*. You follow? The computer will eat it all up, the two will never know, tranquillity will return to the street . . .

I am learning about pain. Went to sleep in my chair yesterday and was woken by a daisy of a one. It seemed to come from nowhere and everywhere, very slowly, just to swell and crowd out everything. Some little shred of mind remained curious. How bad could it get? And then I thought, "Of course, you fool, this must be *it*." So I tried to say "Come in, Death. Welcome," and "Goodbye world, you bastard," but couldn't say anything. Realized my face was all screwed up and my mouth wide open. Silent scream. And then just as slowly as it had come, it went. Left me with such a sense of wellbeing I thought (maybe it's true!) that my medical problem had burned itself out all in one go and I was going to live for ever.

So after that I decided to have a big lunch – did, too (relative to present appetite). But before I got to that, up the path came a young woman and an older man. Recognized the type at once. Evangelists. Usually I don't let them waste my daylight but this time I listened to the usual crap ("When you see a ship down in the harbour, you don't think it made *itself*, do you? So why should you think this wonderful world of ours, the trees, and the grass and the animals . . ." Oh shit!) Well, having listened I thought earned me my turn, so I told them I was already spoken for. Did I mean I was Catholic, he wanted to know. Oh no, I explained it was worse than that: years ago the devil came in the form of a beautiful American woman and told me if I promised my soul to her, I could have all the women I wanted. I said it seemed to me a pretty good arrangement, because I've always liked women and never found a lot of uses for my soul. I mean, it's locked away in there, never does anything, or says anything. You can't clean the car with it . . . So I signed up, and it worked.

They were off down the path before I'd quite finished.

Do you disapprove, Stan? Yes, you're right. Not nice – I shouldn't have done it. It was because of all that shit about

159

the ship in the harbour and did I think the rivets got there by themselves, and the funnels, and the masts . . .

Darling Laurel (and Kiss me, Hardy), this must stop. I wanted you to know I'm cheerful and that I've felt guilty since phoning you and asking you to visit. Forget that. There's no need. I've thought about how you left me up north and that I should take a leaf out of your book. I still remember it – how I noticed a silence and looked around and you *weren't there*! That's exactly how it should be. Thank you for the lesson.

I send you all the love in this shipful of rivets,

Yours (truly),

Maurice

★    ★    ★

"Hullo?"

"Laura? It's Dan. How are you? How's the weather up there?"

"I'm dry. It's wet. How about you?"

"Oh God – you know. Same story."

"Ruth Warner diarizing you into a cocked hat?"

"Absolutely. Look, Laura, I'm sorry to bother you but I feel you should be warned. Television have got on to the Tapler cottage project . . ."

"I know."

"You know?"

"They got in touch with me. Wanted me to show them the property. I said I didn't have a key. They said from the outside would be OK. And would I answer a few questions."

"I see. Bugger them."

"I said I would. Should I refuse?"

"No. They might make something of it if you refuse now. But you should be aware of what's going on. Be careful how you respond to their questions."

"What *is* going on?"

"I'm not quite sure. Have you got a few minutes for me to explain?"

"Of course. Fire away, Danny boy."

"You sound like Vince."

"I think that was supposed to be an imitation."

"Of course. Sorry. Well look, it's like this. I had to be at a dawn ceremony for the lifting of a tapu on some Maori artefacts. At the National Museum. It went on and on – karakias, songs, the usual interminable stuff. Terry Scobie was there with his TV crew so I had time to look at him. It's interesting, you know. He's lost the hippie image. He looks a bit – well, I thought dangerous. Have you seen him lately?"

"No. Not in years."

"He's got that disappointed look. Cheated. The big things never happened, just the big talk and the dope smoke. They're the ones you watch for when you get into Labour politics. They're always out to prove they haven't given up on their principles. After the ceremony he caught me waiting on the steps for my car. Asked would I mind answering a few questions in front of the cameras while they had them set up in the Museum. I'd already agreed to an interview. I understood it was to be some kind of brief portrait at the end of my first year in Cabinet. But it was supposed to happen in my office – Ruth had fixed a time. So what did Terry want with me at the Museum? He said just a few preliminary questions – something they could work on and develop further when they brought the cameras to my office. Are you with me?"

"I'm with you. It does sound the kind of thing that could be a trap."

"Exactly. But I'm such a half-wit. You've probably noticed. I skirt round the little things and fall into the biggest most obvious holes. Not that it seemed there was anything

161

to worry about. They gave me a dusting, stuck me up in front of an ancient carved Maori lintel, and got me talking about current issues. There were a few barbed questions and tense moments, but I thought it passed off well enough. A bit random. I couldn't see how the thing could be shaped. But that was Terry's worry, not mine. So far so good was what I felt. A few days later he was in my office with his team – as arranged. This time they had me in my ministerial chair . . ."

"With the flag behind."

"Right."

"Maori lintel in some shots, flag in others . . ."

"Oh Laura, I should have you down here as my adviser. I guess it's obvious."

"Only because you've told me something went wrong. Who did the questioning?"

"Michael Friend. God, he's such an insect. He wears leather slip-ons with no socks."

"They're very fashionable, Dan."

"Maybe, but there's something so . . ."

"Unctuous?"

"It's that smile. I'd much rather have Perrigo. He might slug you, but at least you know it's happening. Friend's one of those bastards who've thrived on Rogernomics, and on being seen to discredit it."

"So what happened?"

"Well it was quite alright to begin with. And then all of a sudden they dropped the Tapler purchase on me. I'd had absolutely no warning. We hadn't released anything, so no one was supposed to know it was even a possibility. I had to think quickly. I knew if I refused to answer, it might be used against me. Remember the time when Bob Tizard was asked questions that had no relation to the agreed subject of an interview? Did you see it?"

"He walked out, didn't he?"

"Yes, and they just used it – poor old Bob tearing off

his mike and clambering over their gear to get out of the studio."

"So you were trapped."

"That's how it felt. I was hugely pissed off, but I thought I managed quite well. Showed a minimum of surprise and displeasure — even when, as a final thrust, they asked whether it was true that my former girlfriend was involved in the project."

"Oh dear. That was below the belt."

"Certainly was. And it must have come straight from Terry. When it was over and I had time to think about it, I was sure all the rest was subterfuge. The real object of the exercise had been the Tapler project. I don't know what I can do about it. A few defensive measures — including this one. Warning you that it's happening. And I've demanded a transcript of both interviews. I've had the first already. I put a copy in the mail to you. The second should follow in a day or so."

"Do you think it matters? Would anyone really want to shoot down the Tapler thing? I mean writers are hardly . . ."

"I don't think they give a damn about the cottage. Or writers. They're after bigger game. It's just one small shot in Terry's war against the Government. You know he's an Anderton supporter. And he's always had a grudge against me."

"Are you sure, Dan? Sure it's not . . ."

"Ministerial paranoia? I wish it was."

"Can they really do any harm? After all, there's nothing discreditable . . ."

"No, there's nothing discreditable, and yes, they can do harm."

"Simple as that."

"Afraid so, Laura."

"Well, I'll be careful . . ."

"Look both ways."

"Look both ways. And keep my fingers crossed . . ."

"And keep me posted."

"I will. And Dan . . ."

"What?"

"You take it slowly down there. It's not worth killing yourself . . ."

"I will."

"Promise?"

"Promise."


Next day the transcript of the first part of the interview arrived.

## TVONE FRONTLINE

Cooper/Min
  *Prod:* Scobie
  *Loc*: National Museum     *Date*: 6.8.90
  *Int*: Scobie
  JZ7Fro&P

INT:     Minister, you've had a strong radical image. How does that fit with this Government's free market policies?

COOPER:  I agree with those policies.

INT:     Of course, as a member of the Cabinet you're obliged to.

COOPER:  Yes, but I agree with them anyway.

INT:     You must be aware that a lot of people suppose you hang in there because you think it's better to be at the table influencing policy.

COOPER:  If that's so, then a lot of people are wrong.

INT:     But the pain, the unemployment . . .

COOPER:  Just to get it clear, Terry, what kind of thing do you want here?

INT:     Not sure what you mean, Dan.

COOPER:  Do we need to go through all that – I mean the

|          | routine answers? Is that the kind of thing . . . |
| INT:     | Routine or otherwise – it's up to you, Minister. |
| COOPER:  | OK. Well, I hope that's not part of the [inaudible]. OK. Here goes. On the economic question . . . everything's relative, isn't it? I mean Eastern Europe had full employment and the economies were so shaky the people in jobs were poorer than the unemployed are here. Eastern Europe can't be our measure of success, but it's not irrelevant. |
| INT:     | So we just have to put up with it. |
| COOPER:  | In the short term, yes. I mean if some of us sound bored these days rehearsing the reasons for opening up the New Zealand economy, getting rid of protections which distorted the value of everything, putting an end to a system that counted on inflation to render debt insignificant, while in the meantime more debt piled up . . . How did I get into this sentence? What I mean is, yes, that was it – if we sound bored, it's not a lack of conviction. It's the tedium of saying what by now, surely, everyone knows. |
| INT:     | Someone – was it one of the Sir Roberts? – called you Minister for State Toilets. Did you get the kind of portfolio you hoped for? |
| COOPER:  | I was glad to be elected to the Cabinet . . . |
| INT:     | You wouldn't have preferred something else? |
| COOPER:  | What do you suggest? Defence? |
| INT:     | I take it that means you're opposed to the purchase of new frigates. |
| COOPER:  | I didn't say that. |
| INT:     | Are you opposed to the purchase? |
| COOPER:  | No. |
| INT:     | Is that the Cabinet Minister speaking? |
| COOPER:  | This is Dan Cooper speaking, so far as I know. |

INT:      Can you tell me why you support it?

COOPER:   It has to be seen in the context of CER. If we're
          serious about merging with Australia . . .

INT:      You want that?

COOPER:   Yes. We tend to insularity.

INT:      What about the Pacific?

COOPER:   What about it? We're sitting in it. So is
          Australia. It won't go away.

INT:      I was thinking of Polynesia. Can I point out,
          Minister, that just behind your head there's a
          very beautiful and very ancient piece of Maori
          carving.

COOPER:   Polynesia won't go away either. But it's
          changing all the time, and so are we.

INT:      New Zealand independence . . .

COOPER:   Is something very recent. Nationalisms aren't
          sacred. We have to grow up.

INT:      What does that mean?

COOPER:   What do your questions mean?

INT:      I'd like to ask you about the Arts. You're
          known to buy New Zealand paintings, to be
          interested in New Zealand writing. I understand
          you're some kind of patron of the NZSO. But
          where does the Treaty of Waitangi fit in?

COOPER:   I don't know. Does it have to fit in?

INT:      So the Treaty's unimportant?

COOPER:   No. But it's a silly question. Like 'You drink
          beer and eat cheese. Where does the Treaty of
          Waitangi fit in?'

INT:      It's been said that your notion of New Zealand
          culture has become Eurocentric . . .

COOPER:   Drinking beer and eating cheese are pretty
          Eurocentric, aren't they? But of course, if it
          has to be said one more time in 1990, I'll say it:
          the Treaty's a document of historic importance.
          It has to be acknowledged and respected. All

I've added to that is that it's only one element in
the national picture. We can't let ourselves be
handcuffed by it.

INT:     Thank you, Minister. We'll continue with this
at a later date.

END JZ7Fro&P Scobie


*     *     *


In my imagination I've been over it so many times it's like
a memory – so vivid that I am, or anyway my personal
stake in it is, expunged. I see Roger driving along the East
Coast Bays towards Ginny's flat going over our quarrel,
using it to stoke his anger and harden his resolve.

The quarrel – it was because he bought a new BMW
without telling me, "as a surprise" – went something like
this:

"You knew I wasn't keen."

"You didn't offer one good reason why we shouldn't
have it."

"You didn't explain why we should."

"It's a great car, Laura."

"We don't need a great car."

"We can afford it . . ."

"There are other things we could have spent all that
money on."

"Can't I just once in a while feel free to spend?"

"Of course. But it would be nice if we discussed it."

"I tried. You were always negative."

"BMWs are a Yuppie cliché. It's like Vince when I was
a child – always buying Jaguars."

"He was right. They were good cars."

"They were vulgar . . ."

"Oh please, spare me the Anarchist kindergarten talk."

"I wanted a McCahon and you bought that boring
Goldie."

167

"You're sentimental about Maoris but when I buy . . ."

"Nothing to do with Maoris. You bought it as an investment."

"Yes. And as something people who come into the house can *understand*."

"What do they *understand* by a tattooed Maori in a bowler?"

"McCahon's a fashion. A fad . . ."

"The Frances Hodgkins would have been a compromise."

"Hamish Keith thought it was probably a fake."

"And what about the Evelyn Page?"

"You're never satisfied. You criticize everything I do. Other women would be pleased. Grateful . . ."

"I'm not other women."

"You're not loyal, you're not honest . . ."

"What are you talking about?"

"You lied to me about Dan's visit. And what was that stuff you were burning in the garden?"

"I told you – a novel."

"About Dan."

"It wasn't about anyone. It was a novel."

"You didn't want me to see it. I'm not stupid."

"Yes, you are, Roger. Stupid is what you are."

That, I'm sure, was what he wanted – a confirmation, an excuse, a release. He marched out, slamming the door.

As for the rest – I can see that too, as I'm sure it must have happened. He knocks at the door of Ginny's flat and she opens it. "I need to talk to you," he says.

"Sure," she says. "Come in." She stands aside to let him pass. "I was just reading the stuff you gave me on the Equiticorp case."

They go in. "Sit down, Roger," she says, but he can't. He's too wound up.

His memory of students' rooms is of colourful disorder – radical posters, mystical symbols, strings of fine shells

168

that rattled in the breeze, Indian rugs, wicker baskets. Ginny's room, as I imagine it, is all controlled brightness and hard edges – a white desk with enamelled steel legs, an electronic typewriter, a red anglepoise lamp, red sloping trays for papers, black bookshelves holding law texts and (do I allow her?) a single shelf of novels. There's a small white television set angled from the wall so it can be watched from the bed, and beneath it a CD player and speakers. On one wall is a pink Art Deco electric clock advertising piston rings, and on another a steel-framed print of a Hockney swimming pool.

I think it may well be my doing – my fault – that Roger is here. His obsession with Ginny dates from the night I accused him of having an affair with her. I was wrong then; but by speaking it aloud I made the idea somehow admissible, like evidence in court.

Since then the thought of Ginny Scobie has disturbed his nights and unsettled his days. She only has to talk to him for five minutes and he finds himself feeling happy and confident. When a few days go by without seeing her, he becomes restless. But the sense that there's an emotion undeclared between them can't go on for ever. Something has to be done to bring it out into the open.

Standing in her room now, he loses courage. What if she should laugh? Or treat it as a kind of harassment?

"I came to make a short speech," he says. But his courage runs out. "Do I need to make it?"

She shakes her head and says, "No." The word is barely audible. There's no expression on her face, except perhaps apprehension.

He has so prepared himself for a rejection, he assumes she means that what he has come to say will be unwelcome. But her hand is on his arm. She draws him away from the door and closes it behind him. She's standing close to him now, looking up at him. "I know what you want to say," she says.

He nods, grim with emotion and self-restraint. He feels his eyes moistening. This is terrible. She reaches up to touch his head and stands on tip-toe to be kissed.

An hour, two hours, later, I imagine him sitting at the wheel of his BMW looking at the harbour water and the red and green lights of a small boat passing under the bridge. He thinks how people say of someone, "He's a new man", without ever considering it might be more than an empty phrase.

It's as if the world has opened out wide and a long-suppressed self has rushed to fill it. Out there now, beyond the windscreen, is the darkness of the harbour and the brightness of lights on water, the heavy steel beams of the bridge, the murmur of traffic overhead and the faint sounds of music from the restaurant on the old ferry wharf. He can see silhouettes of pohutukawas against a segment of sky, and the lights of a jet coming in slowly towards Mangere. It seems the whole universe is more vivid than it has ever been, while at the same time he can still feel and taste and smell Ginny, and remember her voice in his ear.

★　　　★　　　★

I found Maurice . . . But no. Let me tell this, too, as if it happened to someone else:

Laura found Maurice dozing in his chair, but he woke at the sound of her footsteps on the verandah and seemed alert and refreshed. "Laurelissima!"

He picked up a novel from the table at his elbow. "Stendhal," he said, rather too loudly, waving it. "*The Scarlet and the Black*. Have you read it? You should, you know." He was standing now, not altogether steady, but he took both her hands and kissed her lightly, first one cheek, then the other.

"When I got this – ah . . . what shall we call it? – unwelcome news, I couldn't decide whether to do a crash course in old favourites, or fill in some of the classics I'd missed. Decided on some of each. Strange, isn't it, to read something because you're heading for the exit? But I'll tell you something funny, or weird, or – well, you tell me what it is. I made a list, you see. Thought I must surely have read all of Dickens – nothing to catch up on there – but then I realized I'd somehow missed *A Tale of Two Cities*. So that came first. Of course. Of *course*." He waved his hands in the air, signalling the priority of Dickens among the novelists. "Wonderful book. Don't know how I missed it. Just an oversight. But, OK. So far so good. Next came Stendhal. The bloody old red and the black. *Le Rouge et le Noir*, as we Parisians say. And you know what? They both end with the hero going to the guillotine." He let out a hoot of laughter. "How about that? First Dickens, then Stendhal. Chop, and then chop again. Message, d'you think? Little reminder from the gods?"

She thought he looked surprisingly well. He'd lost weight and seemed keen-eyed and – not handsome, he had never been that – but strangely prepossessing.

He took her by the arm and guided her through the house to a glassed-in area at the back. There were lily pools and paving stones and ferns and fuchsias, and in the centre a table set with bread and cheeses, smoked fish, and a salad in a wooden bowl. There was also fruit, and a bottle of white wine.

"I have to be honest," he said, when Laura expressed pleasure. "Ulla did most of it. Yes. My sometime Swede and erstwhile wife. She comes over and gives me a hand. Keeps telling me I don't deserve it, and it's true. I deserve the big chopper, the eternal guillotine . . ."

"Ulla's married again . . ."

"She is indeed. Jamie's a fine, upstanding, impermeable Trotskyite. Ulla's got a slight hypertrophy – is that the word? – of the left brain."

"She married you twice."

"Something like that. Did better the second time round. But here we are . . ." His hand shook only slightly as he poured the wine. He raised his glass and put on his Humphrey Bogart voice. "Here's lookin' at you, kid."

"You're very chirpy, Maurice," she said, touching glasses with him.

"For a dying man, you mean?"

"For any sort of man."

"I'm up and down. The prospect of you, my beautiful Laura, and now, more than the prospect, the fact, has raised me up."

They smiled at one another like old conspirators. Maurice said, "Ginny tells me your children are little models. Well, of course they are. What else? And you're doing something up at the factory. Waste of time, of course. Terrible place."

She told him about her research on Hilda Tapler.

"Dan's aunt," he said. "I knew her, you know. Not well, but we used to meet sometimes at the broadcasting studios, or Progressive Books in Darby Street, or at Somervell's. Oh, and Brookings too. It was a bookshop in Customs Street – I used to see her in there a lot."

Laura told him she'd picked up on those places. "Somervell's especially. It probably seems strange to you, Maurice, but when you do research on a writer and then you meet someone who knew her . . ."

"I understand. You want my impressions of her . . ." He thought for a moment.

"Impressions. Recollections. Anecdotes."

"I liked Hilda. She came from a stuff' shirt family, you know – naval chaps married to croquet mallets – so in those days I had a built-in prejudice against her. But she was cleverer than the rest of them. Talked straight – looked you in the eye. Tall. Crisp. Quite nice looking. Ngaio Marsh type." He looked into the distance, as if watching her coming into focus. "Intelligence – that was the strongest impression."

Laura agreed. "It's in her journals and letters. I've been discovering things about her private life. You don't figure in it, do you, Maurice?"

"She was a bit old for me. I liked younger women." He looked up and grinned. "Still do."

Laura cut slices of bread. "Her papers are in the University Library; and some in Auckland Public. I've been down to the Turnbull to read what she wrote to people like Sargeson. But Dan and I visited her cottage . . ."

"Ah yes, I went there once. She took me swimming. Had a little boy with her. Might have been Dan."

"It's a lovely place. Just up the hill from where I live. There's a chance it might be sold unless . . ."

Maurice interrupted. "D'you know – I'd forgotten, but it's coming back – I did think once that something might come of my friendship with Hilda. There'd been some little stirrings – a bit of charm, some more pleasant than usual pleasantries. Then there was that invitation. But when I arrived she had the child with her and we went swimming. Had a good talk about books, and I went home."

"You didn't know Dan's father? Or anything about him and Hilda?"

"No. Was there anything to know?"

"The father didn't come back after the war. Dan always thought it was something to do with his other aunt, April. You know Hilda was his aunt Amelia. Well, the point is, it wasn't April. It was Amelia. I think it was probably quite a juicy episode."

"Tell me more."

"I can't, Maurice. Not until I've told Dan."

He nodded. "Good. Don't pander to Scobie the gossip. But speaking of gossip – I mean the world stuff. Have you read this morning's paper? Mother Russia's running short of food and there's talk of the Fatherland sending food parcels." He covered his face, seized with silent laughter. "I don't think even you could understand how funny that seems to me. Not the fact. I mean, as a fact it's nice. Russians are hungry, Germans have plenty, so Germans feed Russians. Good. But the politics – capitalist economy bailing out communist one. I feel as if history has contrived the biggest joke against me it could think up, just to see me off. 'Bye, Scobie old son. Just wanted you to know what a mutt you've been.' And I don't mind – that's what's odd. I'm not gnashing my teeth and asking why I wasted my life. I don't even think I did waste it."

He looked up through the glass of the conservatory, and quoted, not as if he thought it connected with what he'd been saying (though perhaps it did), but just because a patch of blue had opened between billows of white:

> The sun-comprehending glass,
> And beyond it, the deep blue air, that shows
> Nothing, and is nowhere, and is endless.

He shrugged. "I decided to write my memoirs. Think I told you in my letter, didn't I? Didn't get very far. Never was a writer. I'm a reader – writers have to be grateful for people like me. There aren't a lot of us any more. Anyway, I scratched away at it for a few weeks and then thought that's it, finished. The end. A whole life and it was just a skinny little folder. I read it through and couldn't find myself. Wasn't there. No one home. It was just a history of ideas. New Zealand as a colony, which it certainly was when I was young. New Zealand here . . ." He pointed as if to a dot on a map. "And here . . ." indicating a vast area beyond, "the world, its news, its interpretations of itself, its mythology, its literature, all coming in at us. We were lived by history. That's a phrase of Auden's, isn't it? The world flowed through us – through our brains. It's still true.

174

The only difference is, we think all that's changed. We have grand delusions. But you see, I – I mean *I*, Maurice Scobie – had vanished into those vast movements of modern history and modern thought. Of course, I could have told the story of what I'd seen and done, but every time I found myself drifting in that direction I felt embarrassed. Why was it important? When I ate a good meal or made love – that was the best of me, but I wasn't at that moment worthy of special record. I was part of the process. Part of this living surface of the planet that keeps on rippling and breathing and replicating and dying . . ."

"But Maurice . . ." Laura interrupted him. "What about poetry?"

"Ah. Hmm." He looked down at his plate and thought, then looked up and smiled. "Yes, I admit – I thought about that too. There's what I call my memory bank. Bore everyone silly with it . . ."

"Not true. We love it."

"You may love it, my dear. Thousands don't – or wouldn't if they met it. But yes, I thought about poetry."

She liked to hear him say the word, which he pronounced "poitry".

"Reading has been such a large part of my experience. That was something I found disconcerting. When I came to think about my life in detail my recollections were so incomplete, so fragmentary, so faint. Even Spain has faded. And the war in the desert. I know I experienced those things. But now I only have the knowledge, not the memories. Or – that's not quite it: they're like memories of memories. Even my adventure with Lee . . ." He shook his head. "Only childhood doesn't get dimmer. I don't think my memory's worse than most. Better, probably. But so much gets wiped off the slate. I had to face the fact that those novels I was reading – the Dickens and the Stendhal – they were more real to me than most of my own life. And yet they're fictions. I seem to have a twin inheritance, you see. There's politics and there's literature. The politics, you might say, has always failed me; the literature, never. But that isn't getting it right either. It's only the very young who think politics will produce a happy ending, like a romantic story. When you get involved in politics you're just putting yourself into the mincer of history. The handle turns and in due course you come out the other end and discover what kind of sausage it's made of you. Literature's a bit tougher than that – a bit more resistant to the time process."

He took up his fork and picked idly at his salad. "I don't know how Dan puts up with it . . ."

"With politics? I think he's got limited objectives. He'd like to get a few things done."

"I grew up in a revolutionary school. Never mind the petty details, we were going to change the world. I'll give you a little allegory, Laura." He smiled at the recollection of it. "I told you, didn't I, in my letter, about the young couple next door, and the traffic cop across the street? Taking that ticket and paying the fine – it was my rebellion against authority. I felt so pleased with myself. Thought I'd done something great. Beaten the system. But there was something I hadn't thought of. The neighbours didn't know what had happened – that was necessary to my sense of triumph – so of course they went on parking wrong-way-about when it suited them, and a couple of days later the bastard wrote them another one."

She laughed. "Is that an allegory, Maurice, or just a sad suburban story?"

"It might be both, mightn't it?" He refilled her glass. "I'm sorry, Laura. I'm running on. Or running down. But it's been an interesting few weeks. Strange, rather lonely, very intense. Left me in a state of intellectual uncertainty. All I'm certain of now is that I'm sorry to be leaving the party."

"You mean . . . No, you don't, do you. Not the political party."

"Oh no. Heavens. Not the party with a big P – I left that during the ice age. No, I mean the life party. The fun."

"It won't be such fun without you."

"Ah, now, young Laura . . ." He cut two wedges of brie, keeping his eyes down. "Don't be kind to me. It's not good for my composure."

She took the piece he held out on the point of the knife, and helped herself to more salad. "OK. Just to restore your composure – shall I tell you what I thought of reproaching you with?"

"Oh God . . . No, start again. Yes, please – reproach me. It will be good for my soul."

"Are you sure?"

"I'm sure of nothing, my dear, except that you are a sight for sore eyes and you make me regret my age and my infirmity."

She let that pass, and they were silent for a moment while she ordered her thoughts. "It has to do with the time when I was all upset and confused about you and Dan and Roger . . ."

She paused. "Why don't I make it more specific? You remember Terry's friend, Justin Pope? I talked to him once about you. It was after our little adventure up north. I don't know why Justin was the one I talked to, but anyway he was. He listened to all my ramblings and then he thought for a bit and finally he said, 'Tell Maurice to fuck you or fuck off.' At the time it seemed to me crude and unhelpful. But when I remembered it the other day I saw the point."

Maurice grinned. "I wish I had, of course. Not that my generation used that word in the presence of a lady." He reflected a moment. "It's the things you don't do you regret, not the things you do."

"But why didn't you?"

"Ah." He looked up again. The blue was widening. It

177

seemed to be pushing the two piles of white cloud to opposite sides of the frame. "Why didn't I? You mean I could have?" When she didn't answer he clowned, "Vy, vy, vy? Zat is vot I ask myself."

She wanted him to be serious. "Maurice, you're dying, aren't you?"

"Ya, I am, my dear, dyink."

"Then answer me. Next year you won't be around to ask."

He gave it some thought. "I took you to see the bush and the stream and the falls . . ."

"Your sacred place."

"My sacred place. And then . . ." He looked at her. "I don't really know, Laura. It's a long time ago. Maybe I thought you might rescue me from my obsession . . ."

"With Lee?"

"With Lee. She rejected me after Dick left her. Wouldn't see me or speak to me . . ."

"You played with my feelings."

He held his hands open in a gesture of *mea culpa*.

"You both did. You and Lee."

"We were a bad and wonderful pair. Ah, the sex." He closed his eyes, remembering. "But then it got – not just good. It was too good. It was never enough. There are limits to what the body can achieve. When you reach the limit, that's when it gets dangerous. You bring in the mind to add twists, to create entertainments, challenges, obstacles . . ."

He stopped, noticing that she wasn't smiling. "I'm sorry," he said. "What can I say?"

"You destroyed something."

"Between you and Dan? Did we? I suppose so. We also destroyed our own affair. When things are destructible . . ."

There was an awkward silence. Maurice said, "I did harm, played havoc, hurt people. I know it, I acknowledge

178

it, I'm sorry for it. But if I'm honest with you – should I be?"

"Yes."

"I regret the harm, but I don't feel guilt. One hurts and is hurt. It's sheer egotism to feel guilt. You don't understand that, do you? If you live long enough it may come to you. I'm just a fragment of the process, an insignificant speck, an aggregation of cells that have come together and are about to fly apart. There's no 'I'. It's an invention . . ."

She felt tears welling up. He stopped talking, patted her hand, got up and went indoors. After a moment the first eerie soaring notes of Strauss's "Four Last Songs" came winding out. He returned to his seat and they listened.

Laura peeled and divided an orange and stripped away the white pith. The second song had begun before she was able to look up and smile. "That's so beautiful. It would reconcile me to . . ." She waved a hand. "To anything."

He nodded. "Charm on that scale – it's shameless – but it's irresistible."

They listened again, drinking the wine.

"There used to be that Leftist dream of working-class art," Maurice said. "Now here I am devoted to a high bourgeois . . ." But a sudden shower of notes silenced him.

When the last song began he translated the opening lines:

Here in need and in joy
We wandered, holding hands.
Now let's pause at the last
Above the silent land.

When it finished he went into the kitchen and made coffee. Bringing it out on a tray he said, "You know, Laura, I climbed into a lot of beds with a lot of women, but I only took one with me to – to that place in the bush."

179

She nodded a kind of acknowledgement, though she wasn't sure what she should understand by it. He went on, "I thought of it when I got to the end of *The Scarlet and the Black*. When Julien's condemned to the guillotine he thinks of a cave high in the mountains above Verrières where he's had his best thoughts and loftiest moments. He wants what's left of him buried there. It's pure Romantic indulgence, of course – but there it is. The 'I' that doesn't exist goes on asserting itself to the last."

He went indoors and changed the record. It was Strauss again, she recognized that, but not where it came from.

"I've suddenly gone in for technology," he said. "I've resisted it and now, just in the past year, I've got a microwave, a video recorder, a new stereo set and CDs, and I've had a decent aerial put up so I can get Concert FM." For a moment he seemed to have forgotten imminent death, or was setting aside all thought of it. "I've even thought of getting an Answerphone. I don't need it. But you know I'd love to have a message that said – the usual stuff – 'The phone's unattended at the moment' and all that crap. And then, 'If you would like to leave a message please speak after the third fuck off. Fuck off. Fuck off. Fuck off.'"

When it came time for her to go and they were standing at his front door, he asked, "How is your life, Laura?" She must have looked puzzled, and he said, "I suppose I mean your marriage."

How to answer? She smiled and lied, "It's well, thank you. How's your divorce?"

"I like that," he said. "Well done." And then, quickly and briefly hugging her, so that for a moment she felt how bony his frame had become, he said, "Let's close on that note. Goodbye, my very good friend."

Laura swallowed and was silent. He'd made it clear that she was not to come again.

"Say goodbye," he instructed.

She said it. "Goodbye, Maurice."

He nodded and smiled. "You're a good woman, Laura. A soul mate. Never think, later on, that anything was left unsaid. It's all said, and understood. OK?"

"Yes."

"And write me a novel, will you? You can do it."

"I will. I promise."

As she went down the path she noticed that buds were forming on the lilac trees. She turned back. "Lilac," she said.

"Ah yes," he said. "October is the cruellest month."

But that wasn't quite all. When she got home her phone was ringing. It was Maurice.

"I forgot to tell you the latest story out of Russia. They say Gorbachev tells it himself, to journalists. It goes like this. Gorby says, 'Mittérand has a hundred lovers. One has AIDS, and he doesn't know which. Bush has a hundred security guards. One's a terrorist and he doesn't know which. And I,' Gorby goes on, 'I have a hundred economic advisers. One's smart and I don't know which.'"

For a moment she couldn't speak. "That's all," he said. "You like that, Laura?"

She said – in what was probably a faint voice – that she liked it.

"That's all then, darling. Bye." And he hung up.

She put down the phone and sat for a moment, half angry, half amused, her eyes brimming again. That's Maurice, she thought. One moment he says goodbye for ever, the next he's phoning to tell you a funny story.

She wondered whether he was really dying.

★   ★   ★

And about this time the second transcript of Dan's TV interview arrived through the post.

Cooper/Min
  *Prod*: Scobie
  *Loc*: Beehive      *Date*: 10.8.90
  *Int*: Friend
  JZ7Fro&P/2

INT:      You're considered to be one of the dries.

COOPER:   It's a dry time, isn't it?

INT:      That's not an answer.

COOPER:   Yours wasn't a question.

INT:      Would you be happier if Roger Douglas was
          still in the Cabinet?

COOPER:   If he wanted to be, and it was possible . . .

INT:      You sided with Douglas against Lange, didn't
          you?

COOPER:   I regretted the split.

INT:      But you thought the Douglas programme
          shouldn't have been stopped.

COOPER:   It wasn't stopped.

INT:      Slowed down then.

COOPER:   The pace of change is important. The market
          had got hopelessly distorted by Government
          interventions, so I'm convinced the Douglas
          revolution had to happen. Who isn't, apart
          from a few people so far to the left they're in
          danger of falling off the political map? It's not
          a question of the correctness of the theory, but
          only how much correctness a country the size
          of New Zealand can stand in a short space of
          time.

INT:      So you think Douglas went too fast.

COOPER:   Possibly. It wasn't that he was wrong – just that
          you can't sprint in gumboots.

INT:      Now if we can change tack for a minute,
          Minister: we understand you've been pushing for

the purchase of a property in the Eastern Bays that belonged to a writer, Hilda Tapler, who died a few years ago.

COOPER: I . . . No, I . . . I don't think it's right to say I've been pushing for it. I've responded to an idea that's come to me from several sources.

INT: These were?

COOPER: It came first from writers. I understand PEN supports the purchase. Then there were petitions from the local community.

INT: Others?

COOPER: The local Council, of course. The Bays MP has been more than helpful. The Library Association . . .

INT: We understand the locals are chiefly interested in the land attached to the cottage.

COOPER: That, and the idea of commemorating the work of a literary pioneer. I should have mentioned the Spiral Collective. They're a women's publishing group here in Wellington. I think there's a feeling that Hilda Tapler hasn't had her due. She was an early exponent of what these days is called meta-fiction. I don't think there was a word for it then.

INT: Aren't there rather a lot of our writers who might be commemorated in this way?

COOPER: Not a lot, no.

INT: But more than one.

COOPER: Of course. It's a matter of beginning somewhere. We hear so much of Mansfield, and do so much to remember her. But otherwise there's very little – the Sargeson house in Takapuna, Baxter's grave on the Wanganui River . . .

INT: Have you any personal reason for pursuing this particular writer's memorial?

COOPER: A personal reason? I . . . No. Oh, unless you're referring to the fact that Hilda Tapler was my mother's sister. That makes me especially pleased that there's been this move to do something to remember her work. But of course it's not the prime motive . . .

INT: No other personal reasons?

COOPER: No. None at all.

INT: We understand that a woman organizing the petitions is an old friend . . .

COOPER: Ah. You mean Laura Barber. I think it's her husband Roger has done the work. He's a prominent lawyer . . .

INT: But Mrs Barber has an interest?

COOPER: Yes, indeed. I understand she's doing postgraduate work on Hilda Tapler's fiction.

INT: And she's a close friend . . .

COOPER: I know Laura Barber. I respect her work. As for close friendship – I believe I've seen her half a dozen times in twenty years.

INT: So you don't think it's significant . . .

COOPER: What do you mean by "significant", Mr Friend? I could ask, for example, is it "significant" that the daughter of your producer is helping with the petitions?

INT: Yes, true. Probably not . . . Just to alter the focus a little, Minister. What about your Department?

COOPER: What about it?

INT: Is this kind of thing strictly within the ambit . . .

COOPER: There are grey areas between Departments. Possibly the suggestion came to me first because Hilda Tapler was my aunt. But my officials feel they can deal with it, in collaboration with the Arts branch of Internal Affairs.

INT: You agree that Hilda Tapler's work made little impact in New Zealand.

COOPER: It had no great public success here. But she was very highly regarded by her fellow writers – Sargeson, Robin Hyde, Fairburn. Her biggest success came with her only novel, *Nor Question Much*.

INT: And that was in England. Wouldn't it have been better to commemorate the truly New Zealand writers?

COOPER: She was as New Zealand as they come.

INT: You see, Minister, a lot of people are going to think here we are spending public money on yet another Eurocentric ikon when this is our sesquicentenary year, the year when we ought to feel we've come of age as a Pacific nation . . .

COOPER: We'll have come of age as a Pacific nation when we stop going on about it.

INT: . . . and furthermore that the occasion for this expenditure was nothing more than the personal whim of a Minister who wanted to do something for the memory of his literary aunt.

COOPER: When you've been in politics for a while you learn that whatever you do there will always be some who doubt your honesty and impugn your motives. The safe thing is always to say a lot and do nothing. I didn't come into Parliament to do nothing.

INT: Thank you Minister for giving us your time.

END JZ7Fro&P/2

\*    \*    \*

My name was Laura Barber. What is my name?

And now Laura Nameless has to end this account of the dog days with another invention. No, of course I was not there to hear what was said; but something of the kind must have passed between them, and this will do as well as any other. If you don't find it convincing or to your taste, you may invent your own. The only rule is that it must convey the same piece of information – from her to him:

"It's so nice to have you there, Dan. My bed felt empty without you."

"It's nice to be here."

"D'you mean it?"

"Of course I mean it."

"I've been so worried."

"What about?"

"About us. I thought you were avoiding me."

"It's been hectic, with the Caucus revolt, and the new PM, and the election looming. And now TV are after me."

"I know. I don't usually fret . . ."

"Something the matter?"

"Yes and no."

"Tell me."

"I can't. It's too embarrassing."

"Oh, come on, Caroline. You're not embarrassed with . . ."

"I am. About this I am."

"You've got to tell me now."

"I'm pregnant."

"Jesus."

"You see."

"Well, then. That's . . ."

"I'll have an abortion."

"Do you want to have the baby?"

"I shouldn't. I'm 38 and I've got two lovely children."

"But you want to have it."

"Oh God, Dan, I don't want to make your life more difficult . . ."

"Forget about me, for a moment."

"I'd love to. To have your child. But not if you don't want me to."

"I've never fathered a child."

"You must be appalled. I'm sorry."

"Don't be sorry. I'm 50 per cent responsible, aren't I?"

"Fifty per cent exactly."

"No, I'm not appalled."

"I truly didn't mean to."

"I know that. I watch you plugging in that rubber wheel."

"I should have stuck to the pill."

"There's always the chance . . ."

"It's such a relief to have told you."

"I thought you were quiet this evening."

"I've been worried. I thought of just having it terminated and not telling you. But that didn't seem right."

"No, no. I had to be told. It's mine too."

"But you must feel . . . I mean . . . Invaded – don't you?"

"No, I feel . . . Something's creeping up on me, but it's not that."

"What then?"

"I'm not sure. It feels like pleasure."

"Oh Dan. Really?"

"Really."

"Are you sure?"

"Quite sure."

"Let me kiss you. There. Thank you for being so . . ."

"I think we should get married. Would you like to marry me?"

"Oh Dan, you idiot, what a question. Are you serious?"

"I've been thinking about it. Haven't you?"

"Of course I have. But, you know how it is. I can't get it out of my head that I'm poaching. I've always thought of you as Laura's."

"You must have noticed that Laura's married to someone else."

"Yes, but you're still in love with her."

"Do we have this baby, or don't we?"

"Wouldn't you like to wait until the morning?"

"This is the morning."

"Take time to think it over?"

"Who's the doubting one? Yes or no?"

"Yes, for God's sake. Don't you know I was in love with you twenty years ago? I've always been in love with you. Since the Big Bang."

"When was that?"

"Don't you remember? Laura got her hair in a knot and ran off up north. I came back from a lecture and found you leaning out of the upstairs window looking sorry for yourself. We went to bed together. Only trouble was, you belonged to Laura." A long silence, and then, "That's the problem, isn't it? You still do."

"Laura's not having my child."

"That's true. God, I'm so relieved you don't mind. You really don't, do you?"

"Can't you see me grinning in the dark?"

"There is a sort of phosphorescence."

"That'll be my teeth."

"I think it might be your halo."

"I don't feel like sleeping, do you?"

"Not in the least. Dan darling, come closer. Do you . . . Oh yes. Let's celebrate."

# SEVEN

# 1990 – Messages from the Dead

At the Bay, and I Saw in My Dream . . .

Once again I was absent, outside it, present only as the viewer is, watching a movie. But now it was a dream about a man having a dream. The details were complicated, many of them lost on waking. But here I was, a woman in Auckland, New Zealand (the World, the Universe, Space – yes?) dreaming about a man going to sleep I don't know where except that it wasn't Washington DC, and dreaming that he was in Washington DC. His dream began in a mood of excitement and hope for the future, but there were shadows, then dangers, then threats. Soon he was on the run, crossing the border into Mexico. The town was raucous, lawless, indifferent. His enemies were closing in, they were going to kill him, there was no way of escape, they were outside his door, they were breaking it down . . . But the man had one weapon. Somewhere there was the knowledge that this was a dream. He struggled, as one might struggle to get out a gun – and there! – he dragged it to full consciousness. *Wake up! This is only a dream.* He woke. There was a moment of sheer relief, and then the recognition that he hadn't woken in that anonymous place where he'd been sleeping and dreaming, but in the room in Washington DC where the dream had begun. It all lay ahead of him, and no longer a dream . . .

But this was *my* dream – the dream of Laura Nameless sometime Jackson sometime Barber, Mother of Three, Wife of No-one, Author of Nothing except a monograph, oh yes and a letter . . .

Dan carried the letter in his pocket when he went with Caroline to Maurice Scobie's funeral. He'd read it over many times:

Dear Dan,

I should have written long since about my Hildawork, but after our visit to the cottage (which, as I've told you, proved helpful in so many ways) I wanted to finish the personal and family part which I knew would interest you most – so I could be sure what I reported to you was right.

Before I get on to that I'll just say again what I tried to say when I phoned you the day after the Frontline programme . . . but what *is* there to say? Just that it was grossly unfair – to you, and to everyone involved. I felt so angry and hurt seeing our efforts misrepresented, I'm afraid it left me incoherent. The way they cut what I said outside the cottage and misused it upset me so much I wrote a letter of protest. I've had a reply which is bland and dishonest. I wanted to get Roger into action as a lawyer – or one of his colleagues – but he's angry with me (and of course with you) rather than with the programme. He feels we put him in an embarrassing position. And in any case for quite other reasons there's no possibility of getting him to do anything about it – but I don't want to write about domestic matters.

And now the election has come and gone and Labour is out of office. I couldn't get through to you by phone on the night, but I trust you got my message. I don't suppose the defeat was unexpected; but the size of it must have been a shock. At least you retained your seat and will live to fight another day. It's only a matter of time and you'll be back in Government (I give National three years). In the meantime, you can maybe take a well-earned rest – though I'm told that a numerically small Opposition has to work hard to be represented on all the Parliamentary special committees.

But look, Dan, this is not intended to be a personal letter, and if what follows seems rather official – or rather, I think *academic* is what I mean – that's because I have to tread warily between fact and speculation. So excuse the tone, and here goes:

First, I'm sending you a copy of the note I've prepared on the subject of Hilda Tapler and the man she called, in writings both published and unpublished, Peter Corbot. It's really only background to what was going to be my thesis, but important background, and I might keep it as an appendix. I say "what was going to be" because after a long talk with Steve Casey I've decided not to go on with the PhD but instead to write a short monograph – say what I have to say in something like 70 or 80 pages, which is all it needs. Once that's done, which will be soon, I plan to have another shot at writing fiction.

In "The Magic Bagwash" you write about how you once became obsessed with the idea that your father and your aunt April had had an affair which precipitated the break-up of his marriage. You then dismiss the idea as fanciful, because your mother and April went on living together amicably.

I've put this together with a number of items in Hilda's fiction and journals and arrived at what I'm convinced is the correct answer. You were right in your intuition, except that you had the wrong aunt: it was not April who had the affair with your father, but Amelia (or Hildamelia, as I sometimes think of her). I have to admit that I haven't been able to find the name Brett Cooper anywhere in your aunt's papers. There were a few books on her shelves with his name in them, but that happens in every family where books get handed round. But let me first give you a summary of what I've discovered. You will find details, dates, references in the enclosed note – and the basic outlines, apart from the love affair, will be known to you.

When she was in her early twenties Hilda fell in love with the man she calls Peter Corbot. They were lovers, and their affair was kept secret from their families, who knew they were friends but had no idea how far the friendship had gone. They were devoted to one another, and the only reason for not marrying and ridding themselves of the need for secrecy was Hilda's burning ambition to be a writer. She was afraid that if she married and had children too soon it might swamp her and put an end to her writing. She was determined that she would first travel to London; and although it must have been a painful parting, she went, promising to return after one year. She was able to do this because your grandfather paid her travel expenses, and a small allowance.

At first she found London daunting. She suffered loneliness, homesickness and what these days we call culture shock. But as the end of her twelve months approached, things began to go well for her. She'd got to know some writers. The publishers Duckworth were seriously considering a collection of her stories (they later declined them, saying they needed a novel from her first). She met Elizabeth Bowen, who introduced her to John Lehmann, who of course later, after her return to New Zealand, published some of her work in *Penguin New Writing*. It was possibly also through Elizabeth Bowen that she got to know a well-known poet of those years. He read some of her poems and stories and praised them, but then (as she put it) "spoiled the confidence this had given" by kissing her in a taxi.

She felt she was on the brink of success and that although she missed Peter Corbot, she must stay longer. Although none of his letters have survived, it's clear that he protested and wrote urging her to come home. Then he stopped writing. At first she took this silence to be his way of punishing her.

As the weeks went by and another English winter set in, she became less hopeful, or more realistic. The stories were declined, a novel she was trying to write wasn't going well, she began to realize that there was going to be no instant literary triumph; and she was worrying about her fiancé's silence.

Then came the news that her two sisters, April and your mother, Averilda, were to be married in a joint ceremony – April to a naval officer, Averilda to Brett Cooper, a maths teacher. At this point comes a blank in the record – letters and journals from around this time have vanished. So quite early on I began to suspect that Peter Corbot, as she calls him, might have been Brett Cooper, and that when he married her sister Hilda decided to destroy all evidence of what their relationship had really been.

She must have been distressed, but she kept her head. She knew as a fiction writer it would take a long time to discover her own style and subject and method. Like most of the New Zealand writers of that time she was something of a literary nationalist. She tells herself in her journals that although the London literary world is exciting it won't help her write better; and also that, living there, she was removed from her real subject. She'd been reading everything by and about Katherine Mansfield, and I think the Mansfield example persuaded her that it wasn't wise for a young woman writer to push herself too hard and struggle against adversity far from home. Added to all that was the likelihood of war in Europe. She decided she should set herself up as a writer in Auckland and proceed slowly. When she'd made real progress, then she might return to London – something which she did, though only briefly, in the 1950s.

So now we have her return, and the establishment of the cottage, far enough from the family home for independence, close enough for convenience – the place which became, like Sargeson's house in Takapuna, though less famously, something of a meeting place for North Shore writers. Hilda enjoyed their company, valued their work, and took courage from their example. Your grandfather died, and her share of his estate left her, by no means wealthy, but able to live modestly and get on with her work.

Three or four years pass and there's no mention of Peter Corbot. She has friendships with men, associations, probably love affairs; but always there's an obstacle – it seems she's in love with, or obsessed with, someone else, and so can't give herself completely.

Then Peter Corbot reappears. By now the war is raging and New Zealanders are involved, in Greece and then in Crete. Peter is in uniform and in line for posting overseas. There are several meetings, one of which is particularly lyrical and intense. And that's immediately followed by the crucial encounter. The journal reference to it is brief, distressed, only in note form, and part of the page is torn out, as are the pages which follow. But for years afterwards she will refer to it and try to use it in her fiction. Because the uses and emphases differ so much it's impossible to know which is "correct"; and I think she came to believe they all were. They were different but not contradictory ways of seeing and describing the same event.

If Peter Corbot was, as I'm supposing, Brett Cooper, he must have come to tell Hilda that his marriage had been a mistake and that he still loved her. I suppose the separation from his wife caused by his military call-up had made this clear; and if there was a good chance that he would have to go away to fight, he would have wanted to tell her about his feelings. I assume she was pleased, but confused – this, after all, was her sister's husband. She tried to reject his protestations of love and to resist him physically, but her resistance was – what? Ineffectual? Indecisive? Insincere? Simply unsuccessful? She suggests all these at different times. And this subject – this scene – became one she struggled with and went back to, not just for its own sake and its importance in her life, but because (as she puts it in one of those two notebooks we found at the cottage) "it represented that confusion at the heart of human relationships which it's the writer's duty to explore".

After it happened she was angry – but the longer she reflected on it the less she could be sure whether the anger had been with herself or with him. She'd wanted him to visit; and when he came, she'd felt the strength of the old sexual bond. Then there was the fact of rivalry and jealousy

194

between the sisters. In some primitive part of her being Hilda knew there existed the wish to punish Averilda for marrying Brett.

And there was a further complication, which she was also honest enough to face: if the sex had been unwelcome, why had it been so enjoyable?

In all of this personal history of your aunt, you can see the main preoccupations of a number of her stories, and more particularly of *Nor Question Much* (the title of which, by the way, must come from Donne's poem, "The Funeral":

> Whoever comes to shroud me, do not harme
> > Nor question much
> That subtile wreath of hair which crowns my arm . . .

and so on.)

The scene in the novel which Hilda said she wasn't happy with was the crucial one, where Peter Corbot seems to force himself on Sybilla. Hilda wanted it more explicit – she didn't like an element of vagueness in the writing. But her publishers, when they saw her first draft, had warned her about possible reactions – the fuss about some of D. H. Lawrence's novels hadn't been forgotten – so she toned it down. But there are stories dealing with the same episode, where the sex is more frankly described; and if you add the details of those to what the novel provides you get a more complete picture of what happened.

One thing is clear: Hilda deeply regretted the consequences, and was critical of herself, blaming what she called her own "guilty hysteria" for them.

What *he* felt can only be guessed by his subsequent actions. That he left Auckland precipitately mightn't on the face of it seem surprising. He was soon posted overseas. But I get the impression that he volunteered for this, or in some way hastened it. And of course he never returned.

Now then – is Peter Corbot your father? It seems obvious that he is, but how to "prove" it? The dates of the relevant events recorded in her journal entries, and the facts about Peter Corbot, his age, appearance, etc, all fit. And there's another thing which, though again it's not conclusive, helps: there has always been a slight element of mystery in the novel about why Sybilla felt impelled to reject this man whom she loved and desired. He was married, and that might have seemed a sufficient explanation at the time the novel was published; but it doesn't quite match Sybilla's personality. But if we know that he was not only married, but to her sister, then the problem, and the resistance, are more intelligible.

Even so I hesitated to set all this down, until Steve pointed out something that had been staring me in the face for months. I was saying what an unusual name Corbot was. French, I supposed. Steve sort of woke up (he sometimes gives the impression of only half-listening to me), looked over my shoulder at the name, and said "It's an anagram, isn't it?" You can imagine how I felt. It's so obvious, once seen, but I hadn't seen it. Peter Corbot is an anagram of Brett Cooper.

So what became of your father after the war? And did he and Hilda ever meet again? Here I'm on much less certain ground, but there's one item in the papers that offers a clue.

Hilda's trip to England and Europe in the 1950s seems to have been pleasant and modestly successful. She enjoyed it, but wrote surprisingly little about it. However, there's one story from that time which exists only in a rough draft. The handwriting is more than usually difficult and I'm still wrestling with some almost illegible words and phrases. When I'm satisfied that I've made a reasonable transcription, I'll send you a typescript.

It's set in Germany and once again concerns Peter and Sybilla. They're sharing a room in a small medieval town somewhere in the area of the Black Forest. The town has survived the ravages of the war. There's a square surrounded by tall houses with ornately painted façades, and a daily market to which farmers bring produce from round about.

Up on a hill is the castle, reached by winding cobbled alley-ways between tightly clustered houses. A broad river flows through the town, and in the middle of the river there's an island, entirely covered in trees, but with paths, and access-ible from two bridges that cross the river at either end of the island. There are swans on the river, and the houses on either side are reflected in the water. In one of these houses Peter and Sybilla are sharing a room. They can look down at the river; and if they lean out of their windows they can see a round yellow tower where a famous German poet of an earlier century (she doesn't give his name) was locked up for most of his life because, although he went on writing poems, he was considered to be mad.

It's autumn and the leaves are brilliant red and gold and rust-coloured, showering down over the paths on the island where Peter and Sybilla walk each morning before taking breakfast in a café. On the island there's an immense statue representing a composer of German folk songs, and out of his pockets are emerging the soldiers of the Reich. As the days go by and the island trees shed their cover, the dark shape of this statue gradually becomes visible from their window, like something coming into focus. For Sybilla, still traumatized by the extermination camp horrors which the end of the war had uncovered, it's repellent. For Peter it's something dangerous but also fascinating.

The story has a fairy-tale quality – an air of unreality, yet of something based on reality. We're not told what has brought Sybilla to Germany, nor where she has come from, nor what Peter is doing there. He might for example have been teaching mathematics – he works at figures, and likes to devise number patterns (something which makes me think of him as indeed your father!) – but the special quality of the fiction depends more on atmosphere than on fact.

By the end of the story the couple have resolved the tensions of their past and put all regrets behind them. And their individual strengths are demonstrated in the fact that, although they still love one another, they agree they must go their separate ways. He's making a life for himself in this place; she must return to wherever it is they both came from. It's the one story she wrote in which (as she notes on a separate sheet in the same exercise book) there is no reference to New Zealand. But she adds, paradoxical as ever, "this is therefore my most genuinely 'New Zealand' story".

I was puzzled by that until I remembered that she was interviewed by a reporter in London about *Nor Question Much* and was asked what was "especially New Zealand" about the novel; and that her "instant reply" was, "That's for you to say. It's a New Zealand novel because I'm a New Zealander and I wrote it."

Because so much of Hilda's fiction is based on the facts of her life, and illustrates her maxim that she writes, not to invent what didn't happen but to come to terms with what did, I'm of course predisposed to believe that your father was indeed living in Germany in the 1950s and that she went there, spent some time with him, and that they parted on good terms. But I have to acknowledge, especially because of the unusual fairy-tale quality, that it could be just a way of finally coming to terms with the end of her/Sybilla's affair with Brett Cooper/Peter Corbot – a way of imaginatively tidying it up and setting it behind her. I don't think this likely; but I can't deny it as a possibility. And there I have to be content to leave the matter, since I now want to cross the bridge myself, from the streets of fact to the island of fiction.

Well, Dan, that's it. My little monograph should be finished in a week or so and on offer to the University Press. With support from Steve there's a good chance it will be published. I've enjoyed working on her. I've learned a lot. Now I'm ready to put it behind me. But I will feel distressed if the cottage isn't saved.

I wonder whether you know that Alberto Moravia is dead. He died, in fact, round about the time we were talking about those copies of his novels and stories in Hilda's cottage. I've read a lot of his fiction since. I began with *Conjugal Love*, and I could see why you admired it; and why Hilda did – there's so much in it about the psychology of author-ship. While you were talking about it at the cottage I was glancing through her copy, and I noticed (did I mention this?) that she'd marked something about pain and reality; but afterwards I couldn't remember exactly how it went. I've now found it. The writer, Silvio, who is the narrator of the story, has had a terrible afternoon in which he has found himself unable to see any merit in his just-completed novel, which, while writing, he was sure was a masterpiece. Now it's evening and he's walking in the countryside with his wife. She has gone on ahead, and he's seized with a feeling of unreality. He says,

> It came into my mind, all of a sudden, that the only way I could escape from this atmosphere of unreality was by receiving or inflicting pain – for instance by seizing my wife by the hair, throwing her down on the sharp stones of the path, and receiving from her, in turn, a good kick on the shins. In the same way, perhaps I should waken to the value of my manuscript by tearing it up and throwing it into the fire.
>
> These reflections brought me a vivid feeling that I must be mad: was it not then possible to lay hold of one's own, or other people's, existence except through the medium of pain?

I find that peculiarly comforting just now, and there must have been times when Hilda did too.

I'm rambling on. My life has been – well, *awful*, lately, but I won't embark on that. Keep numbering, won't you. (Don't fight your genes!) I suppose, going on experience, I may expect to hear from you next April, if not before. And yes, why shouldn't I be frank with you and say I hope so?

Much love,
Laura.

★ ★ ★

Now to go back, before the election:

"FRONTLINE" (music, tumbling images suggesting keen minds, sharp eyes, hard facts, and then . . . )

"The Pen of my Aunt".

Images of Dan Cooper in his younger days (some, no doubt, from Terry Scobie's personal files).

"This is the story of a man who was once a radical," (Michael Friend smiles his caring smile), "and what he found to do with political power when at last, two decades later, some came his way."

Photographs of the Anarchist coffee bar, of anti-Vietnam demonstrations, of young radicals making speeches.

A news picture of a protest march, a white circle identifying a young Dan Cooper, hair held back by a headband, eager-eyed among the leaders.

"But the pain, the unemployment . . ." a voice says, to which present-day Dan is seen replying, "Do we need to go through all that – I mean the routine answers?"

Another "radical" image, this time in a 1981 protest against the Springbok tour.

Now the Minister is seen against the background of a carved Maori lintel. "Where does the Treaty of Waitangi fit in?" a voice asks. "It's only one element in the national picture," is the reply. "We can't let ourselves be handcuffed by it."

An anti-nuclear protest now – Dan in a group on board a big yacht that is leading a fleet of boats out in an attempt to stop an American submarine from entering Auckland Harbour. This is followed by the exchange in which he defends the purchase of new frigates from Australia.

"So what did this hot-blooded leftist of the 1970s do when he found himself in Cabinet?" Michael Friend asks. "Not a lot, is what his friends say privately. But he did set in motion, or lend his weight to, a scheme to buy for the nation – at the nation's expense – a piece of land and a rather flimsy cottage as a memorial to one of New Zealand's writers, Hilda Tapler. You've never heard of her? Well, you're not alone in that."

Now there are shots of people approached on Lambton Quay and in Queen Street, being asked have they heard of Hilda Tapler. The answers are all negative.

Any guesses?

"She was the netball captain, wasn't she?"

"The British MP who said something bad about eggs?"

Michael Friend's warm smile returns to the screen. "No joy there. So what has the Minister to say?"

A cut to Friend asking, "You agree that Hilda Tapler's work made little impact in New Zealand?"

"It had no great public success here," Dan admits. "But she was very highly regarded by her fellow writers . . . ."

Friend looks out once again from the Frontline studio. "Of course you mightn't have heard of *them* either."

He sighs. Turning now to another camera he continues, "But is there anything to be said against the idea of making this purchase, apart from its apparent randomness in the midst of all our economic woes? Well, not really – unless it bothers you that the woman who wrote over the nom-de-plume of Hilda Tapler was in fact Dan Cooper's aunt, his mother's sister Amelia Henryson."

Now there's a cut to another part of the interview. Dan is saying, "I don't think it's right to suggest I've been pushing for it. I've responded to an idea that's come to me from several sources."

"These were?"

"It came first from writers. I understand PEN supports the purchase. There were petitions from the local community."

"Others?"

"The local Council, of course. The Bays MP has been more than helpful. The Library Association . . ."

One by one, these assertions of support are called in question. A representative of PEN, a young man with spiky hair and an anxious face, agrees that his organization supported the scheme. But he personally was not told that the writer in question was related to the Minister.

"That makes a difference," he says. "I feel we haven't been properly consulted."

A member of the local Council denies that he and his colleagues are interested in Hilda Tapler. "I don't know what she wrote. It's the land that interests us. It runs down to the stream, and there are some very fine trees."

Asked whether he thinks the Government should be buying a park – even a small one – for the local Council he says he doesn't see why not. However, he agrees the matter has become rather complicated.

"I don't think the Minister has been frank with us," the local Member complains. "But that's typical of this Government."

Michael Friend's face returns. His smile is not malicious, only faintly mocking.

"And what of those petitions from local people? They were organized from the home of a local lawyer, Roger Barber, whose wife Laura, we're reliably informed, was an old girl-friend of the Minister in his radical days."

Cut now to Dan saying, "I know Laura Barber"; then to Laura, standing outside the cottage, saying, "Yes, Dan and I were friends back in the early seventies"; then to Dan, "I respect her work"; and to Laura, "I think he's a good Minister"; to Dan again, "As for friendship – I believe I've seen her half a dozen times in twenty years"; and finally Laura, "Sometimes he sends me a birthday card . . ."

Back in the Frontline studio Michael Friend sums up: "So these two are not, they tell us, friends exactly. They just meet sometimes, and he remembers her – affectionately, shall we say, as he remembers his literary aunt. No doubt he recalls the title of the one novel that seems to have earned Hilda Tapler significant praise: *Nor Question Much*. It's clear you shouldn't question much what this Minister does or you might get an answer like this . . ."

And there's a shot of Dan saying, "When you've been in politics for a while you recognize that whatever you do, there will always be some who doubt your honesty and impugn your motives . . ."

"Sorry, Minister," Michael Friend says, reappearing on the screen. "We thought people who spent public money were supposed to be willing to front up and explain themselves to the taxpayer. Maybe we should just conclude by asking a rhetorical question: Was the purchase cheque signed with La plume de ma tante?

"And now to more serious matters . . ."

★ ★ ★

And the day after the programme:

"Hullo, Dan? It's Laura. I just rang to . . . God, what can I say . . . Dan?"

"Yes, I'm here. Well, never mind."

"It's awful . . ."

"It's New Zealand, isn't it?"

"Does it have to be so . . ."

"TVNZ uncovers major scandal."

"So unfair. Such a misrepresentation."

"You get used to it . . ." (Short silence.) "No, that's not true. You don't get used to it."

"That cutting back and forth . . . I'm so distressed . . ."

"Oh heavens, you mustn't be. It's not your fault, Laura . . . Are you there?"

"Yes. Sorry. I just found it so hard to take."

"Forget it. Put it right out of your mind, if it's making you unhappy. Look, I'll tell you something funny. Last night after the programme I had a dream . . . D'you mind me boring you with my dreams?"

"You know I don't."

"Well, it was in a desert. I could hear the prophet Isaiah making a speech to his horse. I couldn't see Isaiah but I could see the horse. When I woke up I could still remember the last part of what the voice said:

> Lengthen ropes and strengthen hopes
> For you will forget the shame of your youth."

"Oh, that's rather lovely, isn't it?"

"It was one of those atmosphere dreams. Almost made the Frontline rubbish worth it. Not something I could tell the PM though, by way of mitigation."

"Is he angry?"

"Not really. Mildly irritated. Resigned, I suppose you'd say. He knows what we're dealing with. If TV want to go for us they'll always find a way. But he's calling for damage control. Wanted to know whether a deal had been made on the purchase. I told him there was an agreement on price, but it was informal. Nothing definite. That's because Ruth Warner's been dragging her feet. He said that was fortunate. It meant the whole thing could be called off. I said I suspected it was Ruth Warner who'd run to Frontline with the story."

"I didn't know . . ."

"He said if you leave scraps around you attract vermin, and that I'd better clean up my camp site."

"Oh yes. Easily said. What else?"

"He wanted to know whether Hilda was really my aunt. I told him she was . . ."

"Yes, but that's hardly the point. She was an important writer. If they'd chosen to bring in expert opinion, instead of those people in the street . . ."

"He wouldn't have been impressed by *if*, Laura. And I had to acknowledge – I should have seen what was coming."

"So what happens now?"

204

"I'm to make it clear to the vendor that the deal's off. Then there's to be a public correction to the press saying that the idea's been floated but no final decision's been taken, and that no purchase is intended before the election."

"But Dan, that sounds almost like the end . . ."

"For the moment, yes, it does."

"And has it done you any harm?"

"With the PM? – I don't think so. So much shit's hitting so many fans . . . The polls are so bad . . . it's reached a point where nothing can make it worse for us. Or better. We're on the way out."

*　　*　　*

On the day of Maurice's funeral the sun shone, the sky was vast and blue and empty. Flax was flowering. Multicoloured bushes and shrubs and trees in the gardens of Old Government House, ranged and stacked, looked over one another's shoulders. The lawns were green and recently mowed. The sun made rainbows in the sprinkler-showers.

The funeral service was to be in the University chapel but Dan and Caroline had arrived early. Dan watched a pair of starlings going up and down the flax stalks raiding the flowers; then a pair of minahs; and finally, only minutes later, the tuis: Europe, Asia, Polynesia, taking their turn at the honey-pot. He reflected that the tuis, as tangata whenua, should come first; then that which came first depended on when you began watching the rotation. The birds behaved as if they understood that spring wouldn't last, and meanwhile there wasn't any choice – the nectar had to be shared.

For a time Dan and Caroline lay on the grass and dozed, feeling that they had come home. When they went back through the chapel building to the Princes Street side a crowd had gathered and was already beginning to move indoors. Dan found himself embraced by a man he didn't

205

recognize and, once clasped, couldn't look at. "Kia ora, Dan," said a muffled throaty voice.

"You too," Dan responded. He could feel a bone pendant pressed against his chest.

Gripped in this bear-hug, Dan looked over the shoulder of his embracer and saw Kiev. She looked different and yet the same – older, broader, her face still pale, freckled, tranquil. Her eyes settled on him. "Hullo lover," she said.

Now the man held him at arm's length. It was Justin Pope. "You've shorn your prophet's locks," Dan said.

Justin moved his face towards Dan's. He's going to kiss me, Dan thought, and turned his cheek.

"Hongi," Justin murmured.

Dan pressed noses with him once and then a second time.

"When did you become a Maori, for Christsake?"

"At the moment of conception," Justin said. "Same time you became a bastard."

They laughed, looking at one another with pleasure. Dan moved now to embrace Kiev. "Nose or mouth?" he asked.

"Don't be provocative," she said. She kissed him and held him close. Her skin and hair were so familiar he felt a shiver run through his body. This, like the Auckland gardens, gave him the sense of a home-coming.

He introduced Caroline. They all three thought they had met somewhere, long ago, maybe more than once, but weren't sure where. Somewhere in the street, Caroline thought most likely, under a peace banner.

Justin's beard and hair were grey-speckled, neatly trimmed and spiky. He and Kiev both wore hand-crafted leather sandals which turned up at the front, like skis. Kiev's clothes were many-coloured and formless. Her hat was white and broad-brimmed – the kind Island women wore along Karangahape Road on a Sunday morning. And now Dan saw that lined up behind them were three teenage replicas, very orderly, very demure, all in sandals and jeans,

206

all wearing T-shirts supporting "Nuclear-Free Aotearoa". They were introduced – Kahu, Tui and Bert.

"We're growing avocados," Justin said. "And tangelos, oranges, kiwi fruit, grapes. We make a small amount of wine."

"We're on an estuary," Kiev said. "Justin wants to start mussel farming. You should come and visit us, Dan. Both of you." She laid her fingers on Caroline's forearm to include her. "We have Zen weekends. There's a barn for meditation and stuff like that."

She looked around. "What a crowd! We'd better go in, hadn't we?" As they moved towards the doors she reached round Dan's back, sliding a hand under his arm.

In the entrance, propped in a corner clear of the doors and leaning on two sticks, an old man watched the crowd moving past. Dan looked, and looked again.

"Vince," he said. "Do you need help?"

"Hullo Danny-boy." Vince Jackson held out his left hand to be shaken. "Just waiting here while Laura parks the car. Not quite back on my feet yet. Had a bit of a – you know – thing. Coming right, though."

Dan patted his arm. "You're looking great, Vince. It's so good to see you."

They were inside the chapel now. The coffin was at the front, and the cross had been removed from the wall in preparation for a secular service. Maurice's family were already in the front rows. Dan recognized Ulla sitting with Terry and his two sisters, their husbands and children. Terry's daughter Ginny was there too. There was no sign of Ros.

"Ros wouldn't come to Maurice's funeral," Caroline whispered. "She hated him."

Dan was wondering about his own capacity for hate. It had never been highly developed; but the sight of Terry looking up at the patterns of sunlight and leaf-shadow moving on the wall made him think how easy and how satisfying it would be to attack him physically, to take him by surprise and, without explanation, bang his head against the stones.

Dan turned his eyes to the pale polished wood of the coffin and gave his thoughts to Maurice.

After a moment he felt Caroline's elbow nudging his ribs. He half turned in his seat to look back towards the doors. Laura was coming in with her father, helping him to a seat near the back. On the other side of Vince, also helping him, was Steve Casey.

"Laura," Caroline said. "It's such a long time since . . ."

★　　　★　　　★

. . . or something like that. Laura imagines Caroline's reaction at seeing her by recollecting her own at seeing Caroline. It was indeed a long time. After graduating Caroline had married a young man who went into the civil service in Wellington, and during all those intervening years their paths had never crossed. Now Laura saw her – familiarly, distinctly, indelibly Caroline, but a mature woman. It was the sameness in difference that was so puzzling – that and the fascination she'd always felt for someone who was like a sister, almost another self, both friend and not-friend, companion and competitor, never-quite-to-be-trusted ally, loved and loving enemy.

Laura had the advantage sitting at the back: she could stare to her heart's content. But now, like Dan, she focused on the coffin and tried to believe the unbelievable – that Maurice was lying inside it.

The first speaker was Jamie McColl, Ulla's second husband. From the pulpit he talked, in the Scots accent that had stayed with him, of Maurice as a soldier of the Left. Maurice had fought in Greece and Crete and in the Desert in a war against Fascism that had to be won. "A lot of us did that," he said, "and for all kinds of reasons. But those with a sense of history and a commitment to the Left honour especially – and so we should – the ones who went earlier to fight in Spain. The Spanish Civil War was heroic, it was tragic, it engraved itself on our imaginations, it brought us to political consciousness – just as a later generation were brought to consciousness by the war in Vietnam. Maurice had been there. He'd fought in those hard battles among the olive groves. That alone gave him authority.''

Jamie's whole oration was along those lines. Maurice had never let down the side, had always been on the street, and not just when the crowds were big and the cause became popular. He'd been there in '51. He'd been there right through the years of Vietnam. He'd been there in '81. In his final years he'd been less conspicuous, and there were some who thought he'd become indifferent, but it wasn't true. Maurice had always been ready to question and argue with party bureaucrats. But he'd never questioned the cause. The cause remained and he'd given his whole life to it.

"I salute the passing of a fighter for the best of causes, a hero of the Left, a great comrade, one who met history head on and didn't flinch. He should be remembered with gratitude.''

Jamie returned to his seat. There was a silence which went on so long Laura began to feel anxious. Then Justin got up. He didn't move to the pulpit, but stood beside the coffin looking down at it. He spoke a few sentences in Maori, the last of which Laura thought she recognized and understood: "*Ma wai ra e kawea nga tohu o era kua makere ki te Po o Tu?*" – Who will carry the flag of those who have gone into the dark?

There was another silence before he went on in English. He spoke of Maurice as he'd appeared to Terry's friends, trying to live an alternative life-style in that Parnell house in the early 1970s. There'd been a time when Maurice had seemed to want to join them – "to become young," Justin said, "by being like us." He'd changed his style of dress and even taken over some of their ways of talking. For a few weeks his conversation had been punctuated with "man". "You're looking great today, man." It had sounded so strange coming from Maurice, Justin had felt embarrassed. Then just as suddenly he'd given all that up. "I was glad of that," Justin said. "In my eyes he recovered his authority when he stopped trying to please us."

Maurice had been a loyal Leftist who heaped scorn on the commissars of the Left. He revered good writing but he'd been savage about writers. He loved women and he was an old-style male chauvinist. Who was going to talk about Maurice Scobie the lover? There were things that couldn't be said, truths that must never be told. Sex had been Maurice's mysticism, his religion.

After more of this, Justin addressed the coffin again. "Maurice. I'm sorry if anything I've said has offended against the solemnity of this farewell to you. But how could I speak of you and let these things pass without a mention? *To manawa, e taku manawa*. Your heart is my heart. How many women have said that of you, or thought it? How many are thinking it today?

"Atua, spirit of the dead, leave your name here with us and fly free now, fly north, go with the godwits, past Reinga and on to your own Hawaiki, wherever that may be. Goodbye Maurice, old friend. *Haere ra*."

Justin sat down beside Kiev. There was another long silence, and then Ginny got up and went to the pulpit. She was pale and beautiful. In some primitive part of herself Laura hated her; and at the same time she felt something that was like sexual attraction, as if she had so powerfully imagined Roger's feeling for Ginny, she couldn't help sharing it.

She was not, Ginny said, going to say more than a couple of sentences. Then she would read a poem that Maurice liked to recite. There was a lot she would have liked to say, but she didn't trust herself, and she knew Maurice wouldn't want her weeping over him in public.

"In fact I want to say only that I loved him . . ." There was a precarious pause, and then: "There were times when he was my father and my mother. And later we just had fun together . . ."

That, she said, was for her the most important thing. But because it was personal it didn't seem enough. And so she'd tried to think of Maurice's life as a story. There were a lot of different ways of telling any story. Jamie had offered one. "If I had to tell it," she said, "it would go something like this: Once there was a man with a very big faith and very little doubt. Every year of his life the faith shrank and the doubt grew. In the end the doubt ate up the faith, and the man was free."

Ending her address, she read:

> Once the days were clear
> Like mountains in water;
> The mountains were always there
> And the mountain water.
> And I was a fool leaving
> Good land to moulder,
> Leaving the fences sagging
> And the old man older,
> To follow my wild thoughts
> Away over the hill
> Where there is only the world And the world's ill
>
> SINGS HARRY

\*     \*     \*

Now Maurice was reducing himself to a smoky smudge of sky and a little boxful of ash and at last, even while I grieved for him, I could feel, in some obscure and perversely

211

satisfying way which might have appeased his still potent
spirit, that the snake was swallowing its own tail, the story
drawing to a close as the dream of the dream woke to that
beginning in which everything lay ahead.

Steve helped me get my father home, and then we drove
to Ulla's house. Of course I might find myself face to face
with Ginny, and I didn't want that; but nor did I think
even the smallest decision should be influenced by such a
possibility. If it hadn't been for Ginny's presence I would
have wanted to be there. Therefore I must go. We would
both, she and I, have the good sense and the civility to avoid
one another.

The house had a broad verandah at the rear looking over
a garden enclosed by trees that dropped away into a gully.
I stood out there with Steve among people some of whom
I knew at least by name. Ulla came out and talked to us for
a while, and introduced us to Jamie McColl. We drank
white wine, and Steve ate what seemed to me a very large
number of sausage rolls.

Through double doors open to the verandah I could look
down a long room and see, at the farther end, Dan and
Caroline in a group that included Justin and Kiev and their
three children. Later, when I looked again, Caroline was
gone and Dan was making his way through the crowd
towards the verandah. I saw him pass Terry Scobie, hesi-
tate, then move on. When he reached us I could see he was
agitated. He greeted us both, and Steve offered him the
plate of sausage rolls.

Dan began to tell me how pleased he was to have my
letter, which he showed me he was carrying in his pocket,
and the three of us talked about what I'd discovered. Steve
told Dan about my monograph, and that it was to be published. They were flattering, or anyway encouraging, about
my work. And then the conversation turned to Maurice.
We reminisced about him, and talked of what had been said
at the chapel.

We were standing slightly apart from the others on the verandah when Terry came out to us. He said it was good of us to come to his father's funeral. It was a statement proper to the occasion; but he kept his eyes towards mine and Steve's, avoiding Dan's, and I felt it was one of those intuitive things a person who is in the wrong does – using an opportunity to neutralize Dan's hostility.

Dan must have felt it too. He said, "Your father rang me after the Frontline programme."

There was a moment while Terry decided how he should respond. "I don't think this is the time to talk about . . . differences, is it?"

But Dan went straight on. "Maurice said he wanted to apologize for his offspring's vandalism – that was his phrase."

Terry bristled. "Bullshit," he said. And then, in a more controlled tone: "This is a funeral, Dan."

"If you want protection from the truth," Dan said, "stay away from me. Your father thought you were a trivial little shit, and so do I."

"I suggest you leave," Terry said. But when Dan stood his ground, he moved away indoors.

How did I react? As anyone would, I suppose. I was embarrassed, disapproving – most of all shocked. Steve was staring at the ceiling, his head tilted at such an angle it looked as if he'd had a terrible accident.

The awkward silence continued, until Dan said, "I'm sorry to have inflicted that on you two."

Steve shook his head and moved his hands in signals that were the equivalent of "Not at all"; but the sense of an embarrassment persisted.

"There's a certain satisfaction," I admitted, "in seeing a Scobie savaged. It's just as well we didn't go on the offensive together."

I could see that he didn't know what I meant.

"I guess I'd better leave," he said. And then to me, "You haven't spoken to Caroline."

"I saw her with you," I said. "So you're friends. Close friends? Hasn't she gone?"

He said she was lying down.

"Headache?" I suppose my smile was faintly mocking. "Too much cucumber?"

Dan didn't smile. "You were never fair to Caroline," he said.

I hadn't expected that. "I'm sure that's true," I said. "On the other hand I don't suppose I'd want to attack her at her father's funeral."

We looked at one another. God, I thought, you're so *familiar* – even (or especially) when we're on the edge of a quarrel.

"Caroline's fine," he said. "She's pregnant."

No, I hadn't been ready for that; even less for what followed.

"I meant to tell you," he said. "We're married."

I must have said something in reply. Afterwards I remember only that I stood with both hands on the rail, looking down into the trees and thinking, So this is where the dream ends, feeling a perverse sense of pleasure at the pain of it.

*       *       *

My name was Laura Jackson also known as Promising Beginner, and when the One Great Scorer came to write against her name He wrote not that she won the Game but that she lost concentration, because she had no wish to be a champion at tennis, nor at anything else, but rather a longing, long suppressed, for the game of tongues and "the intolerable wrestle with words and meanings".

My name was Laura Barber, and only the One Great Scorer as He speaks in the future through the thoughts and actions of three children will answer how well or badly she played that Game, but she thinks it will be fair if He says that she gave it her best shot.

My name was and was not Larissa Vincent and when the One Great Scorer came to write against her name He could find no trace of it in His records but only a whiff of smoke and a shower of ash blowing across a suburban garden.

What my name will be on the fiction-writer's title-page is undecided but for the moment I favour L. J. Vine (two initials and a monosyllable – there are precedents for such economy), and what the OGS will say of her through the "blind mouths" of publishers' readers and over-worked reviewers will be, if she is lucky, no worse than the usual self-contradicting babble, and she will learn to be thankful, as her mentor-from-the-shadows Hilda Tapler was, even for their smallest mercies, knowing that once you start down that path it's like the Pararaha Valley – there's no turning back.

★   ★   ★

"I've been through your proofs, Laura. Just a few things to check with you. What about tomorrow morning?"

It was Steve Casey, and the proofs were of my monograph on Hilda Tapler which the University Press was to publish.

"Oh Steve, that's kind," I said. "But don't you think I should stick to the new rule – mornings for the novel?"

"Yes, of course. I forgot."

"Evenings are best – once I've got the kids to bed. But how does that suit . . ."

He laughed. "It sounds great – if you trust me."

"Oh, I trust you," I said.

"Tonight, then? About 8.30?"

"Yes – that's fine."

"So I'll see you . . ."

"Before you go, Steve – do you remember the quotation on Katherine Mansfield's grave?"

"'But I tell you, my lord fool . . .'"

"That's the one. '. . . out of this nettle, danger, we pluck this flower, safety.' You don't know where it comes from, do you?"

"I think one of the *Henry the Fourth*s – Part One, probably. I'll check the Concordance and ring you back."

"Would you? Do you mind?"

"No problem. 'Bye for now."

I put down the phone. Steve had surprised me by approving of this shortcut with my work on Hilda Tapler. And now he was encouraging me to try once again to write a novel.

My central character, I'd decided, would be a woman in her late thirties. Should she be called Larissa? Or why not Lara, as in *Dr Zhivago*? Or Laurel, emblem of victory and therefore daughter of Vincent? Or Lorelei, who sat on her rock at the Bay and sang to passing sailors? Or Jo, like the crossing-sweeper in *Bleak House* (I'd always wanted to be Josephine)? Or Thumbelina who married a toad? Or Liberty, because she would be free; would recognize no rules; would discover her own limit? She might even lay waste – or was that too ambitious? Lay *modest* waste, I thought; and I jotted the word down – "modest" – because it amused me.

My divorce was going ahead – painfully, though I wanted it now. I felt something less than hatred – more like extreme distaste – for Roger. I was still assailed by moments of jealousy and rage, seeing him, as I sometimes did, driving by with Ginny. There was also fear, not of anything in particular, just at the ending of something that had gone on so long.

I was glad Maurice had made me promise to write a novel. He must have known it was what I wanted to do, and that I would help myself achieve it by letting a promise

216

made to a dying man seem solemn and binding. It made me efficient. I worked hard to clear the decks; then worked hard at writing. So far there was only a random pile of sketches and notes – I had still to decide where it should begin. But if it had, as yet, no shape, it was at least giving a shape to my life.

The phone rang and it was Steve with the answer to my question. The quotation on Katherine Mansfield's grave came, as he'd thought, from *Henry the Fourth* Part One. Act II, scene iii, line 10. I thanked him.

"See you this evening," he said.

On a pinboard to one side of my desk there was the only item from Hilda Tapler's papers which I hadn't mentioned to anyone, and intended to keep. It was a photograph of a grave, somewhere in northern New Zealand, almost certainly the Hokianga. In the background could be seen cabbage trees, a single pohutukawa, an arm of the sea, and across the water, glaring white sand-hills. On the headstone was engraved

KATYA LAWRENCE

1888–1954

*But hark you, Kate:*
*Whither I go, thither shall you go too.*

So there had been a grave, a headstone, and therefore a woman, "Katya Lawrence". That much was no invention. I was going to pursue this question no further. My monograph was done, and Hilda's Mansfield story mentioned only as a late fictional idea, left, like so many others, uncompleted. That was what I had written, because it was what would be believed. But for myself . . .

In my volume of Shakespeare's Histories I looked for and found the play, the act, the scene, the lines that John

Middleton Murry had had engraved on the Mansfield head-stone: "But I tell you, my lord fool, out of this nettle, danger, we pluck this flower, safety."

I read on through the scene. It was between Kate and Hotspur. Kate was pestering him to tell her what plans were afoot. I let my eye run over the lines, trying to imagine why Murry might have chosen that quotation. I'd almost given up, when at the end of the scene came the lines,

HOTSPUR:     and for secrecy,
          No lady closer; for I well believe
          Thou wilt not utter what thou dost not know;
          And so far will I trust thee, gentle Kate.
KATE:     How! So far?
HOTSPUR: Not an inch further. But hark you, Kate:
          Whither I go, thither shall you go too;
          Today will I set forth, tomorrow you.

The lines came as a shock. "Kate" on the gravestone was surely Katherine, the two were one, and the quotations on the two headstones at opposite ends of the earth had been taken from opposite ends of the same scene.

It was as if I'd had a message from beyond the grave, but in such a form that it could go no further, except by another such indirect and subterranean route as the one by which it had reached me. I felt I'd been meant to receive it, and to pass it on; but that it should never be "public" – and if I'd tried to make it so I wouldn't have been believed. Katherine Mansfield and Hilda Tapler were dead; and where the line had been drawn in their lives between fact and fiction was more than ever uncertain. It was an uncertainty I was meant to live with, and to make use of. "Thou wilt not utter what thou dost not know"; but one knew other things than verifiable facts.

I got up and walked about the room. I looked out over the roof-tops towards the Gulf. There were yachts on the water sailing out past Rangitoto. I felt an urgent need not just to make notes and sketches but to make a real beginning, before full summer arrived, bringing with it Christmas and school holidays.

I changed into walking shoes. I needed to think more precisely about this, and walking always helped.

A brisk breeze was blowing scuds of high white cloud over the suburb. A shadow raced over and was gone, followed by another, and then another. Between and around them the light was bright, picking out every detail clear and sharp.

As I climbed the hill I could hear bulldozers and chainsaws. I went in that direction, still thinking about my novel. The chainsaw whined and grumbled, accompanied by the crash of falling branches. The bulldozer lumbered and bashed. There was the sound of timber smashing and glass breaking. I knew before I got to it what I would see. The last wall of Hilda Tapler's cottage was bending and breaking as I rounded the corner. Most of it lay already in smashed pieces around and under the caterpillar tracks, while in the background a swathe was being cut through the trees, all the way down to the stream.

I stood at what remained of Hilda's fence, and watched. There were still patches of the old garden. I went in and broke small branches from flowering bushes and scented shrubs – rosemary, lavender, daphne, verbena, kumara hoe, autumn glory, several fuchsias, a red-flowering manuka, a white bush daisy – thinking I would plant them in my garden to make a small memorial to the writer.

A workman came towards me – he looked like a foreman – removing his earmuffs. "Noise driving you mad?" he asked. "We'll be finished tomorrow."

I nodded. It was all I could manage as I watched the bulldozer push down the last wall of the cottage. I could see its inner lining – some of that island matting which Hilda had nailed down with battens of half-round.

"There's going to be six nice town-houses down there," the man said. "We're putting a drive down through the trees."

I felt blank. My thoughts would attach themselves to nothing except the shape and feeling of the novel I would write. I thought of Dan's attempt to make a story of that past time. That could be part of it – but we couldn't be left, as he had left us, romantically marooned under pohutukawas, like the lovers on the urn.

"Everything comes out white." Of course it didn't; it came out black. But in some mysterious way, that absurd motto was also true. Wasn't it Maurice who had said the universe was self-correcting? So it was. But he hadn't mentioned how painful the corrections tended to be.

Back at the house I put the slips from Hilda's plants into a jar of water. In the evening, after their meal, the children and I would make a bed for them in the garden. It would be one project for the summer, to get them established, water them and keep them growing. The little garden could be given a name – they liked that sort of thing. Angela and Ben could choose it – something to remember Hilda by.

I went to my typewriter, still moving in a state so passive it felt almost like a trance, and wrote, "My name is Laura Vine Barber, 26 Rangiview Crescent, Eastern Bays, Auckland." That was all – no more than a practice at the keyboard. But though I would have admitted it to no one, I knew it was, at last, a beginning.

Now it was time to collect Jacob from the crèche.

The boy next door had put a record on his stereo. The suburb seemed to throb and bump with the bass notes and the drums. That will be a problem, I thought, but the thought came without anxiety. Beyond it, in the distance, I heard a great crash as a tree fell.

A gust of wind ruffled papers on my desk. The phone rang and I walked across the room to answer it.